Spring Break in Savannah with A Gangsta

O'Sharra

"Everyone has a price. What's yours?"

-Blessen

Chapter One

"That'll be \$2,132.25; how will you be paying? Debit, credit, or ACH?" the medical billing collector from Emory Winship Cancer Institute asked Bryshere politely as if she had asked him for twenty dollars instead of two thousand.

Reaching into his wallet, he pulled out his debit card as his hand shook nervously and tears filled his eyes. He had worked his ass off for weeks and saved every check, barely spending money on gas for his car and food to feed himself. He'd been saving this money for his tuition for the last two semesters at Clayton State University. Two more semesters until he officially had his bachelor's degree in political science. Two more semesters until he could apply for his dream job in the mayor's office. The starting salary was six figures, and after completing the unpaid internship last summer; he had all but been promised the position after he graduated.

"Hello, Mr. Durden, are you there? How do you want to pay the balance?" the woman persisted.

"Yes, I'm here. I would like to pay by debit card.

"Thought we lost connection for a moment," she joked. "I'm ready for the card number whenever you're ready."

Taking a deep breath, Bry read off the numbers on the front of the card as well as the expiration date and security code.

"And the zip code for the billing statement?" the biller asked nicely.

"30310," Bryshere replied as tears fell from his eyes.

"Perfect, your payment is complete. Thank you so much for entrusting Emory with the care of your grandmother, Hattie Mae Durden. I will send the receipt to your email address on file," she finished before ending the call. Not bothering to reply, Bryshere threw his phone on the passenger seat of his beat-up Honda Accord and laid his head on the steering wheel.

Since he was three months old, Bryshere's grandmother, Hattie Mae, had raised him. Late one night, Hattie had gotten a call that her son and his girlfriend had been taken to jail for a home invasion a few hours after they'd dropped off their infant son to her, pretending they were going to the movies. Both of his parents had been sentenced to life in prison for a robbery that claimed the life of one of their accomplices. They were young, dumb, and reckless. Bryshere's maternal grandmother was ashamed of his mother's actions and despised his father. Even as a baby, Bryshere was his father's spitting image, so she didn't deal with her grandson. His paternal grandmother had loved him unconditionally. Instead of looking at the baby as a burden, she looked at raising him as an opportunity to start over with the son she'd lost to the system and do better.

Better was exactly what she'd done. Bryshere was a good boy. Unlike his father, he hadn't given her any trouble growing up. He helped her around the house, worked hard in school, and got a full scholarship to his first-choice college, Clayton State University, when he graduated from high school. His father hadn't made it past the eighth grade. The only thing his grandmother didn't agree with was his relationship with his high school sweetheart, Bria. Hattie felt that they were too young to be so serious. She didn't agree with the fact that they'd been together since their freshman year of high school, and they were going off to college together. Sure, Bria was a good girl, but their love reminded his grandmother of the bond that Bryshere's father had with his mother, and you see where that had landed them both — in jail for life. Sometimes, young love could be dangerous, and Hattie didn't want history to repeat itself.

Things weren't perfect, but life had gotten exceptionally harder when Bry's grandmother was diagnosed with throat cancer when he was nineteen years old. Two years later, at seventy-four years old, his grandmother was still fighting her battle with cancer. Even though Hattie Mae received Medicare benefits through the State of Georgia, her radiation treatments, medicine, and routine doctor visits weren't completely paid for by the state. That was where her only grandson Bryshere came in. He'd been working overtime to pay for his grandmother's medical expenses. When his grades slipped drastically due to more working than studying, he lost his scholarship, which added the pressure of paying for school in addition to the mountain of debt he was incurring while trying to keep his grandmother breathing.

He knew a man wasn't supposed to cry, but he broke down in the parking lot of his job because he saw no way out of his situation. His pride wouldn't allow him to ask his girlfriend, Bria, for help because she had already helped him out so much. She'd been paying for their dates, putting gas in his car, paying for his car repairs when something went wrong, as well as feeding him. He knew that she truly loved him; he was her first everything. However, Bria was no longer that shy, brace-face, ninth grader he had a crush on and approached in the school hallway. She was now a brown-skinned, full figured, smart, and very beautiful nineteen-year-old young woman who turned heads whenever they stepped out. She'd been riding with him through these tough times, and he prayed that she wouldn't grow tired of seeing the potential he had and give up on him and their love.

After crying his eyes out in the car for his entire break, Bryshere fired up the rest of the blunt that his coworker had given him and smoked his troubles away. He didn't usually smoke or drink, but he enjoyed the relaxing feeling that a good blunt of gas gave him during times of high stress. He finished the blunt, threw the roach outside on the ground, and emptied the contents of the ashtray. He had never been in trouble, and he didn't want to go to jail behind something as simple as a small blunt of weed. Rolling down his car windows to let the smoke from the car air out, he reached for his cell phone to call and check on Bria.

"Hey, babe," she answered, laughing loudly as the music played in the background. He knew she had to be at her part time job at Hooters on Roosevelt Highway. A Nursing major at Clayton State University, Bria Malone was intelligent and had always made good grades. Her perfect grade point average was the reason behind her scholarship paying for her tuition, room and board, as well as her books and equipment for school. She had only picked up a part time job so she could pay the car insurance on her Volkswagen Beetle, her cell phone bill, and her other womanly necessities. Lately, with all of his financial issues, Bry had become one of the "womanly necessities" she had to take care of. However, she never hesitated when he needed her help. Growing up in the foster system, love didn't come easily to Bria. It had taken a while for her to let her guard down, but when she fell for Bryshere, he had complete access to her heart and all of her resources. Anything that was hers was his as well.

"Hey, beautiful, how's work going?" he greeted her. He didn't like the fact that she worked in an environment that showed off her sexy figure. She would always tell him how men hit on her at work when she walked around with the skimpy orange shorts and tight white tank top on. However, he couldn't deny that she was making amazing money at her job, and sometimes, she came home with tips rivalling what Magic City strippers made in a night. He couldn't talk shit about a job that was not only helping her out but helping him as well.

"It's going," she replied excitedly. "Tell me why this nigga just gave me three hundred dollars, and his tab was only $58.09? That's damn near a $240 tip!" she yelped excitedly.

"When you get off work, go home and put on something sexy. I'm taking you out tonight," she told him flirtatiously. He was happy for her, but a little envious at the same time. Working at Subway, he made $9.50 an hour, and he never got any tips. She had been taking him out so much, he was beginning to feel like less of a man. Whenever he would tell her that he didn't want her to take him on a date and she should spend her money on things that made her happy; she would reply that taking him on dates was what made her happy.

Knowing that it would be pointless to argue, he agreed to the date. They talked for a few more minutes before he locked up his car. He then headed back inside of the sweat shop he called a job and counted down until his shift was over so that he could spend time with the love of his life.

"Go ahead and order what you want, babe, it's OK," Bria told Bryshere as he looked over the menu at the seafood restaurant. A few hours after their phone conversation, they were sitting across from each other at Larry's Crab House because it was Bria's favorite place.

"I told you, I only want some wings," Bry lied through his teeth. He appreciated having a good woman, and he wasn't a leech. He couldn't control that Bria constantly asked him on dates, but he could control what he ordered on the menu. He wasn't selfish enough to get the most expensive thing on the menu on someone else's dime. His grandmother had raised him better than that.

"Yeah, ok. I been fucking with you since I was fourteen years old, Bry, I know you better than you know yourself. You're just trying to order the cheapest thing on the menu so you won't run up the tab. Oldest trick in the book. I'm telling you to get what you want; it was a good tip night for me. Plus, we have something to celebrate. Your girl just aced that hard ass precalculus test I've been studying for!" she bragged while twerking in her seat.

Bria was a sight for sore eyes in a neon green, long sleeved mini dress and a pair of neon green, white, and grey Air Max sneakers. Bryshere loved the fact that his wifey could look sexy as hell dressed down or up. Her long hair was curly and split into a middle part because he loved the middle part on her. Her makeup was applied lightly since it was a Tuesday night, and they were having dinner at a local spot, not anywhere too fancy. Bry matched her fly in a pair of baby blue, grey, and white Jordans that she'd purchased for him when she'd gotten her check last week. He wore the matching blue, grey, and white Jordan shirt, a pair of white distressed jeans, and completed the look with a baby blue and white fitted cap.

"No, seriously. I had a tuna foot long on my lunch break," Bryshere lied, barely able to hold eye contact with her. He'd always been a terrible liar, which was a good trait to have in a boyfriend.

"Ok, I won't press," Bria gave in, as she called the waiter over. After ordering the Fisherman's Feast for herself, she ordered wings and French fries for her boo.

Since they were regulars at that restaurant, the waiter slipped Bria wine, even though she wasn't twenty-one years old like her boyfriend. The waiter knew that Bria and Bryshere were college students. They didn't look like the type of young couple that got into trouble, so he bent the rules for them slightly.

A few minutes into their date, Bria brought up the real reason she'd wanted Bry to come to dinner with her tonight. She knew that it would take convincing, but she had hope that he would see things her way. He loved her, and her happiness was his main priority. She knew that he would do anything to see her smile.

"I need to talk to you about something," she began while taking a sip of Moscato from her wine glass.

"Oh shit, babe. You aren't pregnant, are you?" he questioned, looking afraid.

"That last time we fucked, I pulled out. It was your little freaky ass requesting for me to "put it back in while you were cummin'". I knew that shit was a bad idea. My grandma is going to kill my black ass. We can't afford to have a baby; we're already struggling," Bryshere began to spiral, even though Bria hadn't even opened her mouth to confirm or deny a pregnancy.

"I'm not pregnant, fool," Bria laughed loudly while holding her stomach. One of the things she loved about Bry was the fact that he kept her laughing. He was funny as hell without even trying to be, and she could tell that he was genuinely afraid that she was pregnant. He'd created an entire scenario in his mind just off of her telling him that she needed to talk to him.

"That is not funny, you had a nigga over here about to have a heart attack," he replied, laughing and taking a sip of his Corona with relief. He wanted to have children with Bria, but this was the definition of the wrong time. He didn't have a penny to his name and had no idea how he would feed himself. He couldn't imagine having to figure out how he would provide for another human being. Besides, he wanted to do it the right way. He wanted Bria to be his wife before he made her a mother.

"You were about to give yourself a heart attack that wasn't my fault," she laughed as she wiped the tears coming from her eyes. "Can you be quiet and listen now? Or do you need to make up a few more scenarios?" she asked him jokingly.

"No, tell me what's up with you," he smiled, showing his deep dimples and pretty teeth.

Temporarily lost for words, Bria's heart fluttered. It had been six years with Bryshere. Six long, beautiful years, but she was still as crazy about him now as she was the first day she laid eyes on him in the hallway of South Atlanta High School. Time had been good to him. No longer scrawny and awkward looking with a head bigger than his body; Bry had grown taller and muscular. He now towered over her four feet, eleven inches with his six-foot frame. Aside from his brown eyes, his smile always made her panties moist and butterflies fill her tummy.

"Ok, this is the thing. You know my roommate, Journey, is from Savannah, Georgia. Her family lives there, and last year, she invited me to go home with her for spring break, but we had that scare with your grandmother. I knew that you wouldn't be up for it, and I didn't want to leave your side. This year, your grandmother is doing better. My twentieth birthday is next week, and I was wondering if —"

"No, it's cool, baby, you don't have to ask my permission to go to Savannah with your friend. I'm not that type of nigga. I want you to enjoy yourself and enjoy your birthday," Bry told her hurriedly. He knew that her birthday was coming up, and that was another reason why he was upset as he paid his grandmother's hospital balance earlier. This would be the second birthday in a row that Bry wasn't able to get Bria a gift, even though she went out of her way every year to make his birthday special. Last year, he'd been dead broke and depressed for his birthday. Bria swooped in, sparing no expense. She bought him a nice Nike outfit with the shoes to match, paid for his barber to cut his hair, took him to a restaurant he had been wanting to try, and bought him a gift as if she hadn't done enough. He'd been eyeing the latest Apple Watch six series, but that motherfucker costed more than he could afford to spare. As they ate dinner and talked, she slid the gift-wrapped box across the table and looked away coyly. When he opened the box, he jumped up and down like he'd just hit the lottery. She'd made him so happy for his day. He was glad that she was going out of town with her friend, because at least he wouldn't be around when she woke up on her birthday with no gift from him.

"You didn't let me finish. She's inviting her boyfriend, and I want you to come as well. It's going to be so much fun, and the house is gorgeous, babe, look at it," she told him excitedly as she pulled out her phone and scrolled through it to find pictures of the quaint, three-bedroom house that was a stone's throw from Savannah Beach. Journey's family made good money renting the home out as an Airbnb whenever they travelled.

Bria had grown up in Atlanta, but as a foster child, she was never taken on vacations. She'd aways wanted to go to the beach, but she never got the opportunity. Journey had moved into her dorm last year when she transferred from Georgia State University, and the girls had become close over time. Journey had tried to convince Bria to go to Savannah with her last year, but

Bria couldn't leave Bryshere while he was going through such a hard time with his grandmother. Hattie's primary doctor had told Bry that his grandmother's health was worsening, and she wasn't responding to the treatment. There was a very real possibility that she was about to die. He'd even urged Bryshere to go ahead and begin to make preparations for her funeral. Last year, Bria spent her birthday in a hospital waiting room because Bry was too upset to leave his grandmother in the hospital alone. When a new steroidal treatment was introduced to Bry that Medicaid didn't cover, the doctor asked him if he wanted to put Hattie Mae on the medication and cover the costs out of pocket. Bryshere agreed with no hesitation, and since then, he'd been working overtime to afford the treatments. By the grace of God, the cancer treatments had been helping, and his grandmother was doing a lot better. Bria hoped that Bryshere would be fine with going away with her for spring break this year. Savannah was only a few hours away from Atlanta, and from the pictures Bria had seen, it looked like a beautiful place.

"I'm sorry, baby, I know your birthday is coming up; I just can't leave my grandmother for a whole week. Plus, you know how funny my money has been looking, trying to pay for these meds. I can't do it, but I want you to go and enjoy yourself," he told her while reaching for her hand.

She allowed him to grab her hand while she tried to convince him.

"Bry, your grandmother has been doing better, and Savannah is only three hours away. You'll have your car; the minute something goes wrong with grandma Hattie, we can be on the road to come back. As for money, Journey's parents and little brother are going to Cancun, so she'll have the house to herself. Me and her have agreed to buy groceries; we won't go to any restaurants. We'll stock up on beer, liquor, and wine at the house, and the beach is free. We aren't paying for anything besides gas to get us there. There is absolutely no reason you can't come with me," Bria persisted while trying to get Bry to see her point of view.

As much as she had sacrificed for their relationship, she couldn't believe that he wasn't being more open minded.

"It's not that simple," he retorted stubbornly while rubbing the back of her hands.

"Well, make it simple," she snatched her hands from his grasp.

"Babe," he began before she cut him off.

"No, listen to me; I don't ask for much from you. I give freely, and I don't ask for shit. It's my birthday, and in all of my nineteen years on this earth, I have never been to a beach in real life. Last year, you didn't get me shit for my birthday. I went all out to make sure you enjoyed yours."

"You couldn't wait to throw that up, I see. So, you expected me to buy you a gift and take you out while saying to hell with paying for my grandmother's radiation therapy?!" he yelled loudly while standing to his feet, causing all the patrons in the restaurant to turn towards their table. It looked like they were acting out a scene from *Love & Hip Hop*, and Bria was embarrassed as hell, but her anger overpowered her embarrassment. Standing to her feet as well and not giving a fuck about the crowd Bria continued,

"I didn't expect a gift or a date. You did what you could, and that was at least spend time with me. I'm asking for you to do the same thing this year except in another city, and you're acting like I'm asking you to move mountains." Tears filled her eyes and spilled over to her cheeks.

"I would if I could, babe. I want to give you the world; I just can't afford to right now," he made one last pleading attempt.

"I'm not asking for the world. I'm asking for you to compromise. Maybe that's too big of a sacrifice for you," she told him solemnly. Opening her purse, she dropped a one-hundred-dollar bill on the table and turned and walked out of the restaurant with her head held high. Maybe she had been doing life wrong, trying to take on the burdens of someone else instead of being selfish and thinking about what was best for her. She decided that she was going to Savannah next week to bring in her twentieth birthday with sand underneath her feet and seagulls flying above her head. If Bryshere didn't want to be a part of that, she would see him when she returned to campus.

Chapter Two

Later that evening, Bria told her roommate everything as she cried her eyes out. "After all I've done for this nigga, he has the nerve to not want to come next week. I'm not asking him for anything besides him, and he's acting like I'm asking him to wine and dine me," Bria complained as she wiped her tears from her face and rubbed her wet hands on her pajama pants. Bry was all she knew; she didn't want to start over getting to know a new guy. This was the worst argument they'd ever had, and she hoped that she wasn't about to lose him.

"Let me just call and apologize," she cried as she reached for her cell phone.

"Got me fucked up. Give me that damn phone," Journey took her cell phone from her hand. A true city girl, Journey reminded Bria of the rapper, Light Skin Keisha, who played the character, Brushandria in *Power Book 2*, because of the way she looked and acted. The color of a caramel- coated candy apple, Journey was thick in all the right places, had a pretty face, and had no problem switching a nigga out when he got stupid. Her new flame was Liam, a mixed boy from Kansas, who was the star golf player for Clayton State. He'd recently finished first place at the Bearcat Classic tournament and even made the Fox 5 news. He was definitely the next Tiger Woods. Bria believed that Liam had finally tamed the beast in Journey because she'd been dating him exclusively for the past few months, and Journey was even inviting him to her family home. Things were definitely getting serious with them.

What Bria loved about Journey was the fact that she knew

her worth. Journey wasn't fucking all over campus and creating a name for herself, but she was dating. If a guy didn't meet her standards, showed her that he only wanted her for sex, or didn't treat her the way she deserved to be treated, she had no problem tossing their ass in the waste basket. Her mother and father had been married for over fifteen years, and her mother gave her the game early. Don't waste your beauty, youth, and all you have to offer on a man who doesn't deserve it. Journey was educated, but she didn't hesitate to get ratchet if need be. She was the first female that Bria had ever really opened up to about anything. Living with a person had a way of creating bonds, even if you were each other's polar opposite. Bry had noticed that Journey dated a lot and warned Bria not to get to close to her. Bria was a grown ass woman and didn't give a damn if Bry wasn't too fond of Journey's dating style. It was 2022, and women were allowed to date whom and how often they wanted. She didn't see anything wrong with her friend not tying herself down with anyone until she was sure of him. She admired her for being brave and not jumping on the first nigga that showed interest and getting stuck with him like she had done with Bryshere all those years ago. Even though she loved him, sometimes she felt that her loyalty to him was stifling her.

"You did absolutely nothing wrong, and I'm not taking your side because you're my girl. I'm on the side of right, regardless of who the person is, and you know that's how I was raised." She walked over to the refrigerator and grabbed a bottle of Stella Rosa from it before reaching for a wine glass so she could pour one for Bria.

Even though she had no interest in women, she couldn't help but notice how Journey's ass cheeks peeked from the bottom of her boy shorts. Her friend was bad as hell, and even when she was chilling in their dorm with a crop top, her hair in a messy bun, and no makeup, she was still killing shit. Bria thanked God that she was confident in her sexy curvy figure and her beauty because being around a chick like Journey could definitely make a weak bitch insecure.

Walking back over to her friend's twin bed with the filled wine glass in her hand, Journey handed Bria the glass and sat back down on the edge of her bed before she continued.

"I see no problem with riding for your nigga. Hell, my mom has been with my daddy since before I was born, and he hasn't always had a check. There were times when she was the sole provider and the breadwinner when he wasn't on top, and he told me that that was how he knew she was the one. Some women are so used to a man spoiling them, the moment he can't, they take off for the hills, and that shows a nigga that you aren't loyal. That isn't the case here. You have shown Bryshere that you're willing to ride with him at his lowest. You're there in every way he needs you, and you're a damn good girlfriend to him. Any other girl your age, beautiful, fine like you are, so much going for herself, would have been cut ties with him. I would have told his ass, 'hit me up when you get your shit back straight'," Journey joked while holding an imaginary phone to her ear like she was making a call, while making her voice sound funny. Bria went from crying to laughing at her roommate's antics. It was funny because it was true.

"Jokes aside, though, there's nothing wrong with holding your nigga down. The problem is when holding him down becomes enabling, and you begin to lose yourself in the process. Like in this situation, you have worked damn hard this semester to keep your grades up. You just passed a test in the hardest course on your course load. You work your ass off as a waitress while still maintaining the perfect GPA. Most of these students' only job is to go to school while their parents take care of their every need and desire, and their asses are STILL failing. You've overcome a lot of shit. A lot of people who've come from where you have don't even make it to see their eighteenth birthday, and you're approaching your twentieth. I don't care how much you love a nigga; you have to love yourself double that amount," Journey schooled Bria.

Liam will just have to be the third wheel. We'll party, go to the beach, eat at a bunch of restaurants, and I'm going to show you around my city. I promise, you'll come back feeling so refreshed, you'll be glad that you decided to put you first," Journey assured her and handed her a Kleenex so she could wipe the tears from her cheeks. She nodded her head and grabbed the napkin while wiping her face. Thirty minutes later, there was a soft knock at their door. They'd gotten off of the conversation about Bry and began to watch a scary movie while drinking wine and eating popcorn.

"I know her ass is going to be the first to die because the scariest people always die first," Journey commented on the character as she stood to her feet and headed to get the door.

"Yes," she opened the door with an attitude, placing one hand on her wide hip.

"I need to talk to Bria," Bryshere requested nicely. In his eyes, Journey was a female version of his roommate. His dormmate was a football star and was fucking a different girl in their dorm every other day, but that had nothing to do with him. Birds of a feather may have flocked together, but when you had your own mind, a person couldn't persuade you to do shit you didn't want to do. Bry had never cheated on Bria, and no matter how many hoes his roommate brought into their room, he wasn't tempted. He knew what he had and who he was in love with.

"Hold on for a second. Let me see if she's available." Journey closed the door and turned to Bria, "Are you available, babe?" she asked her sweetly.

Bria smiled at her roommate's protectiveness.

"Of course I am, silly, let him in." She took a deep breath and ran her fingers quickly through her weave.

Opening the door, Journey stepped to the side, "Bria will see you now," she told him playfully while waving her arm in a sweeping motion like a maid.

"Well, thank you receptionist lady," Bry retorted playfully, causing all three of them to laugh hysterically. Going into the bathroom to slip into something to cover herself, Journey left the room to allow Bria and Bryshere time to be alone.

"I brought your food," he told her, handing her the to go bag from Larry's. She grabbed for her food and went to take it into the kitchen.

"Thank you for bringing it over," she told him while she waited for him to finish what he had to say.

"Look, Bria, I love you and don't think I don't appreciate everything you've done for me. I don't want to make you unhappy, but I really can't make the trip with you next week for your birthday. I can't afford to be off work for an entire week. That's a week's worth of pay that I won't get, and I'm already behind with my tuition repayment plan that the school has put me on. I'm just going through a lot, and I'm not really in a partying mood, so I can't make it this time, but I'll make it up to you," he told her sadly.

"You came all the way over here to disappoint me again?" she asked him angrily.

"Let me stop fucking with you. What time are we leaving? Hell, I haven't been to Savannah Beach myself, and this trip is about to be lit!" He jumped up and began to rotate his hips like a male stripper, causing Bria to scream and hit him playfully. He'd tricked her into believing that he'd come all the way to her dorm just to turn her down again.

He laughed and kissed her. After she stormed out, he had time to think about what he was doing. He would be a fool to allow his girlfriend to go on a trip with her fine ass friend, who had no problem dating multiple niggas. He trusted Bria, but there was no way he was allowing her to leave him for a week to go to a well-known college spring break spot, after they just had the worst fight of their relationship. Like his grandmother always said, he may have been born at nighttime, but he wasn't born last night. She had her own mind, and she wasn't a follower; but anger could cause a woman to do some shit out of spite. All those ingredients were the perfect recipe for disaster.

Chapter Three

"That will be \$2,132.25. Would you like for me to add that to your tab, Mr. Harris?" the sales rep at Gucci asked Blessen as she brought him over another glass of champagne. He hesitated before responding because he was trying on a pair of Gucci loafers that he was contemplating adding to the two shirts and belt he'd already picked out.

"Add these to my tab. These are clean right here," he replied, turning his foot from one side to the next and admiring the pattern of the shoe. The sales rep giggled and placed the glass on the table next to him. She walked quickly to the register to add his shoes to the purchase. All she could think about was the extra \$500 this sale would add to her commission next week. She almost hadn't come to work today because she wasn't feeling so well, but something told her to come anyway. God was good, because now she didn't have to make arrangements to pay her rent. Her salary with this commission added was more than enough to cover the rent and the late fee. When Blessen came through to shop, he was guaranteed to "bless" a bitch. He never spent less than five racks whenever he stepped foot in the Gucci store on Rodeo drive.

Blessen Harris was a made nigga. At thirty-four years old, he was the owner of Blessen and Co. Realty. He owned and sold lavish homes all over the world, but he was born and raised in Savannah, Georgia. He'd lived in all of the major cities, Atlanta, Miami, Houston, and he owned a penthouse in Los Angeles that he was headed back to when he finished shopping. He had a place to call home in each of those cities when he wanted some action, but he preferred the calm and quiet of Savannah, and it would always be home. He couldn't wait until his business was concluded so that he could head back to his mansion. It was where all his real memories were. All of the memories he'd made with his wife and two-year-old child before they died in a fatal car accident five years ago, tearing his entire world apart.

"Yeah, those clean right there, nigga. A little too preppy for my taste, but you into that kind of shit," Huncho told him when he glanced briefly over at the shoes then went back to scrolling through his Instagram feed full of big booty strippers, who looked nothing like the plain jane woman he'd given his last name to.

"Nigga, you are twenty-five years old. You can't live in Timberland boots and Nikes forever. These shoes are on that grown man shit," Blessen schooled his protégé and right-hand man while laughing.

"Nigga, grown is a mindset, not a pair of shoes. I've been grown since I was feeding myself at twelve years old. You go ahead and get those ugly ass shoes that cost the same amount as somebody's rent. I'm going to cop me a pair of those Gucci sneakers to wear to your fancy party tomorrow night, and that's all the dress up you're getting out of me. I'm thugging as usual," he replied while shrugging his shoulders. The only way Blessen would get him in a suit was if he was laying in his casket. Even then, if he put him in a suit, Huncho would come back and haunt his ass. While some men wore a suit effortlessly, other men just didn't look good in them. Blessen was the type of nigga that could look good in a three-piece double breast suit or a pair of Amiri jeans, a hoodie, and some sneakers. Huncho left all that classy looking shit up to his best friend and stayed in his lane.

"Oh shit! I have to find something to wear to the Red Affair! It slipped my mind. I was in here buying shit just because," Blessen lied, knowing he was pissing off Huncho, who was ready to change clothes, get business handle, and find a strip club for some pussy to dig in. Whenever they were away on business, he got the opportunity to cheat on his wife freely, without worrying about a hoe running her mouth and snitching on him like they did in Savannah. Every year for the past five years, Blessen threw a Red Affair because it was his favorite color. All of his rich and famous friends, whom he sold real estate to, came out to the party and got a firsthand look as he unveiled all the new properties, he was putting on the market. It was an excuse to throw a lavish party that he wrote off as a business expense. Why would he send out an email blast of every new property he had acquired when he could collect a list and show all the properties at once?

"You know what? I'm gone. You go ahead and spend another three hours shopping like a bitch. I'm about to go and get me some pussy." He stood to his feet with one shopping bag in his hand and headed out of the door. Blessen laughed hysterically. He loved to annoy Huncho. They had been getting on each other's nerves since they met in grade school. Blessen had taken a liking to the young boy's style and looked at him as the little brother her never had.

Standing to his feet, Blessen buttoned the single button on his tailored suit and stuck his hand in his pocket as he walked over to where the cashier was checking him out.

"Just put it on the card that's on file and email me the receipt, beautiful. That nigga got the patience of a three-year-old," he flirted with the sales associate. She nodded, smiled, and put a long strand of blonde hair behind her ear as she processed the transaction through his online account. He was a valued store member because of the amount he'd spent in the store over the years. When the transaction was approved and she hit the button to send his receipt, she handed him his bag over the counter. She was a cute white girl, but he didn't fuck women outside of his race. He was a black man, and he loved black women. His friend, on the other hand, was a pussy hound, and he didn't discriminate. Huncho would fuck any race of woman as long as she had a fat ass. His standards were purely superficial. He'd been that way all his life, and Blessen knew he would never change. Why he'd decided to create a life with a bitch the total opposite of the type of women he fetishized was a question his best friend didn't have the answer to.

Grabbing his large shopping bag, Blessen walked out of the store and checked his cell phone. He had three missed calls from Luciano, his plug. Blessen dialed the number back hurriedly, knowing it had to be important. His million-dollar real estate company was a cover up for the fact that he was the biggest supplier of pills in the south. He had everything from hydrocodone, oxycodone, codeine, and ecstasy. He was the pill man of the south, and his prices were unmatched. He used the profits from his illegal empire to purchase land, property, hire and pay the best architects to modernize and design the homes, then sell the million-dollar homes to the rich people who could afford them. He rubbed elbows with politicians, doctors, engineers, entertainers, rappers, singers, and athletes because they were all his customers. Everybody who was anybody had known or heard of Blessen Harris. Born addicted to codeine before he could say his name, his mother was a crackhead who had turned her life around when Blessen was five years old. He had one younger sister. They were fifteen years apart, and Jam was his heart — the only family he had left when his mother relapsed after being clean for over ten years. The last time was her last time, and she overdosed on a fake Percocet tablet that was laced with fentanyl. It was ironic that Blessen grew up to push the same shit that had killed his mother, but he'd always told himself that he didn't make her take the drugs, just like he didn't make the rest of his customers take drugs. He simply profited off of something they would be doing whether he sold it to them or not.

"Talk to me, Luciano," Blessen greeted his supplier. They had been doing business for over ten years now. Blessen was introduced to him through a friend of a friend when he was dealing pills on a smaller scale. When he met Luciano, they hit it off instantly and began to deal directly with each other — no more middlemen were necessary.

$$\infty\infty\infty$$

A few hours after his meeting, Blessen rested comfortably aboard a private jet, only occupied by him, Huncho, a flight attendant, and the pilot. The lights were dimmed on the plane, and the flight attendant sat in the very front on her cell phone. Going home so soon didn't sit well with his best friend, who was currently snoring loudly across the aisle from him with his mouth wide open, but Blessen paid him very generously to be his bodyguard, so the money came before the hoetivities he wanted to embark on.

"Bring my food stamp card, nigga, before shit get physical," Huncho mumbled in his sleep, causing Blessen to laugh and shake his head. His best friend had been talking in his sleep since he was young. Blessen had heard the craziest things come from his mouth, and not all of them were comical. His wife used to tell him that people with a guilty mind said things they were unable to say out loud during waking hours during their sleep. As much as Huncho cheated on his wife and the mother of his children, he had to have admitted to it during slumber once or twice. However, his wife was one of those "I don't care what he does in the streets, as long as he knows where home is" type of women, who usually ended up with AIDS because what their nigga did "in the streets" rarely just stayed "in the streets".

Blessen didn't understand the reason his best friend cheated, she was a beautiful girl. Even though she was young, she didn't party or hang with her girlfriends. She took amazing care of him and his children, always putting them before herself. Huncho took care of her and made sure that she didn't have to work, but that was only to keep her ass locked up in the house like Rapunzel. He didn't want her to catch him outside being a thot, so he kept her pretty and caged. Shaking his head, Blessen looked out of the window and watched the dark clouds surround him. He was in the prime of his life, and he was making more money than he ever had. There was nothing he couldn't buy himself. He vacationed when, where, and how often he pleased. He wore the finest designers and didn't bat an eye at the price. He drove the newest luxury cars and had an extensive car collection at every home he owned. The women flocked and were willing to give him anything for his attention, and yet, he had never felt so alone. Unhappiness consumed him like a tumor that couldn't stop spreading, and like Solange had said in his favorite song, "Cranes in the Sky", he couldn't out fuck, out shop, or outrun the emptiness.

He rarely slept at night because dreams of his dead wife and daughter plagued his unconsciousness.

"I miss you, baby," he spoke to the clouds as he flew through them. The dimmed lights in the jet and the lights surrounding the plane made it easier to see outside. It was the reason he loved to fly at night more than in the daytime. When Blessen looked to his right, Sabrina was sitting in the seat that Huncho had previously occupied. He knew that he had to have been dreaming, but he didn't give a fuck. Whenever his wife visited him in his dreams, he relished in the opportunity to see her living, breathing, smiling, and laughing instead of cold and lifeless like the very last time he'd laid eyes on her. Her body was so mangled up when he went to identify her and their daughter in the county morgue; they had to have a closed casket funeral. He had a custom gold-plated casket built for her and their daughter, big enough to fit them both and send them to glory like the Queens they were to him. White horses carried them through the streets of Savannah as a marching band followed like a true New Orleans styled homegoing. That was where his wife was born and raised before she left her hometown to attend SCAD, the Savannah College of Art and Design. That was how they'd met. She had opened up a small interior decorating company and was making a name for herself as the best in town when Blessen approached her to decorate a home he was selling.

"Walking down memory lane again, I see," Sabrina told him with her thick accent.

"Our memories are all I have left," Blessen replied solemnly as tears filled his eyes.

"Not for long," she smirked at him before she dissipated in smoke.

"Wait, baby, don't go. Please baby, don't leave me. I need you. Please come back, Sabrina!" Blessen begged her as he tossed and turned, waking himself up from the dream. When he opened his eyes, he looked over to where his wife had once sat, and Huncho burped loudly, scratched the side of his neck, then continued to snore. Blessen looked down at his Rolex that he busted down and filled with diamonds. The time read 9:15 p.m. They had boarded the plane at five p.m., and the plane ride was only five hours, so they would be landing in the next forty-five minutes or so. The dream had felt like forever, but he'd really only closed his eyes for an hour. Laying his head on the Boeing 757 window, he allowed the tears to flow freely down his face as he replayed every single memory he had with his wife and child. He was a man of great wealth, but he would give up every single cent for the opportunity to hold his wife in his arms again.

Thirty minutes later, the flight attendant checked on him to see if he needed anything and notified him that they would be landing in fifteen minutes. Blessen knew that the plane had already begun to descend because he felt his ears popping to adjust to the altitude. Standing to his feet, he leaned over and shook Huncho awake. His ass had been sleeping since they sat down on the plane. He was only resting up so he could get into the streets as soon as they touched down in SAV. It was spring break week, and the city was full of college girls that he could have fun with before they headed back to campus. It was Huncho's favorite time of year and the only time the action came straight to his doorstep instead of him flying across the world for it. The only reason he stayed in Savannah, besides being near his best friend, was because it was quiet and a good place to raise a family. Every day he wished he had Blessen's life because the world would be his playground.

"Let's go to Shanghai on the beach and get some drinks. A nigga well rested and ready to fuck the city up," Huncho told Blessen as he walked over to his Mercedes truck.

"Nigga, we just touched down. Go home and spend some time with your wife and kids," Blessen retorted as he took his bag and threw it in the backseat of his Audi.

"Her ass ain't expecting me home until tomorrow morning, but my boring ass homeboy wanted to come straight home, so here we are. Technically, I'm still in Cali." He spread his long arms wide, causing Blessen to laugh at him. Truthfully, Blessen wasn't getting any rest any time soon, so he could go for a drink on the beach and enjoy the beautiful night.

"Cool, let me go home and get out of these work clothes. Make sure you get a room because I know your ass is going to find a young hoe to fuck on, and you ain't bringing that shit back to my house." Blessen hit hands with his best friend before going over to his car and jumping in the driver's seat. It was a Friday night, and their usually quiet city was buzzing. He didn't feel like sitting in the house alone and spiraling out of control, wondering what the hell Sabrina meant by "not for long" when she came to him in his dream. Did she mean he was going to die soon? Or was he just tripping from being too tired? Either way, he didn't feel like wallowing in self-pity.

"Meet you there in an hour." He honked the horn and sped off the Tarmac, headed in the direction of his house.

When he pulled up to his mansion, he punched in the gate code number, causing the large iron gates to open up and greet him.

He had lived in this house for eight years, but every time he pulled up to that gate, it was like his first time seeing it. The beauty of the mansion was jaw dropping, and he had so many offers to sell it; but there was no way he was leaving this house behind when it was the last place his wife and daughter had called home.

The ride over the winding bridge to get up to the house was almost ten minutes long. The bridge sat on top of a lake and was surrounded by a beautiful, green garden. The entire thing was illuminated, so you could see the beautiful view while driving to the house. When he finally made it to the front door, his live-in maid and butler greeted him.

"You're home early. How was your trip, Mr. Harris?" the maid asked him as she reached for his overnight bag and suitcase.

Henrietta had been with him for ten years, and over that course of time, she had seen him at his best and absolute worst. She was like the mother he never had. She was always willing to go above and beyond for him and always offered a listening ear whenever he needed a woman to vent to. Originally from Warrenton, Georgia, she was a country woman with a full head of grey hair, and she loved to make Blessen soul food. He had to hit his in-home gym every night for at least an hour to keep his six pack, because of Henrietta had her way, he would be as big as his house. She put so much love into her cooking that whenever she made him something, it didn't sit on his plate for five minutes.

"It was amazing. You have to let me take you to California with me next time I go," he replied while taking off his jacket to give it to his butler. Raymond had only been with him for a few years, but he was just as loyal and dedicated as Henrietta.

"Now you know you ain't getting her country ass to go outside of Georgia," he laughed, causing Henrietta and Blessen to laugh as well at the truth in his statement. Henrietta had never been outside of Georgia in all of her fifty years of living, and she had no desire to see the world. All of her children were grown and in their own world, and she found happiness in taking care of other people. His daughter, Terica, had been like a granddaughter to Henrietta. The little girl was her pride and joy and kept her busy. Sabrina practically had to fight with the woman to take care of her own daughter, especially after the baby was first born. Henrietta took it hard when Sabrina and his daughter died, but she stayed strong so Blessen could have someone to lean on.

"You in my business, Raymond. Like the kids say, don't do that, bruh," Henrietta chortled, causing all of them to laugh harder at her attempt to sound young.

"Y'all are a mess," Blessen laughed as he headed up the large, winding staircase to his master bedroom.

"Would you like for me to get some dinner on the stove for you?" she yelled behind him.

He turned back to look at her from the top of the staircase. "No. I don't need you to get my anything, just relax. I'm heading out to grab a drink with Huncho. Technically, I'm still in California," he mimicked Huncho, spreading his arms wide, causing both of them to laugh at him.

After taking a long, hot shower in the glass, stand up, big enough to fit ten people, Blessen dried off and put his dirty linens in the empty waste basket. He then went over to his walk-in closet, grabbed a short sleeve Gucci logo T-shirt, a pair of Diesel jeans, and slipped into his Gucci GG Rhyton sneakers that were covered in the old school brown logo. They'd just dropped from the spring collection and weren't even in the stores yet. He loved exclusive shit. After spraying on some Dior Sauvage cologne, he grabbed the keys to his Tesla and headed out the door to meet his friend.

Traffic was crazy because of all of the visitors in town, and a fifteen-minute drive had taken him thirty long minutes. After giving valet the keys to his whip, Blessen walked into the lounge and restaurant, Shanghai on The Beach. The beachfront hotspot had only been opened for two years, but it had rave reviews because of its perfect mixture of night club, bar, and five-star dining. Usually, a night club had terrible food, even if the atmosphere was lit, but this place offered the best of both worlds. When you first walked in, there were ice sculptures, a large dance floor full of people, and a DJ in a booth in the air, directly over the crowd. Further back, there were tables to dine, smoke hookah, and they had an outside terrace with tables that sat directly on the beach for people who wanted to enjoy the music, get some night air, and eat some delicious seafood. Their crab étouffée was the best he'd ever tasted, and he ordered it every time he came. Heading straight to the back to grab a table, Blessen spotted Huncho on the dance floor with a girl. Dressed in a crop top, coochie cutting shorts, and high heels, the girl was definitely a knockout.

The DJ mixed Bia's "Whole Lotta Money" in with her new song, "Can't touch this", and the girl Huncho was dancing with began to show out. She was throwing her ass in all kinds of ways, and he could hardly keep up. They were practically fucking on the dance floor. This nigga didn't give a damn who saw what he was doing and could possibly report back to his wife at home. He was simply living his best life. When Blessen noticed that all the tables were occupied, he shook his head in annoyance.

"Raggedy ass, broke ass college students," he mumbled under his breath as he went over to an empty spot he found at the bar that had an extra seat next to it. Grabbing the barstool next to him for his best friend, he called the waitress over and ordered a Hennessy on the rocks for himself and D'ussé with coke for Huncho. He sat the D'ussé in front of the empty seat, so that other people would know that the seat was occupied. He didn't know how long he would stay out tonight since his usual table was being used. He decided to at least have a drink and grab some food to go since he'd come all this way. Even though he was in his early thirties, Blessen felt old ass hell sitting amongst goofy, teenaged college students. He hadn't had pussy in a while, but he would never stoop as low as to fuck an eighteen-year-old just to get his rocks off. There was too much grown pussy available for him. Maybe it was because he had a younger sister in college, and whenever he looked at these young girls, he saw Jam's freckled face.

Bryshere turned his nose up at Journey. She was out on the dance floor of the lounge she had dragged them to, practically fucking a nigga with her skimpy ass shorts on. She was acting like it was her birthday instead of Bria's as she guzzled shot after shot. A part of him wanted to take a picture to show Liam that this was the type of girl he was in a relationship with, but he knew that wasn't his business. It was Liam's own fault that he couldn't make the trip at the last minute due to an injury. The day before the group of four was set to depart from Atlanta, one of Liam's teammate's golf clubs flew from the boy's hand and went straight upside Liam's dome. By the grace of God, he didn't have a concussion. However, the team's doctor wanted to keep him in Atlanta for observation. He was stuck in the dorms, being watched over while his boo was in the club acting single. Watching Journey in action, Bry knew he'd made the right move by bringing his ass along on the trip. If it had been him hurt, Bria wouldn't be in the club shaking her ass. His wifey would have canceled the trip to stay by his side.

Chapter Four

The trio had planned to spend a quiet night in the house after sightseeing all day, but Journey convinced Bria to bring her twentieth birthday in right. They all got dressed up and came out to a lounge she recommended. Bryshere had been stressed when they decided to go clubbing. He'd previously discussed with his girl that he didn't have the funds to do anything that wasn't free. Bria told him that he could chill at the house for the night while she and Journey had a girls' night, if that would make him more comfortable. He couldn't watch her every move from the comfort of the house, so he immediately got on the phone and texted his manager at Subway. He set his pride aside and asked the older guy for a one-hundred-dollar loan to take his girlfriend out for her birthday. By the grace of God, Mr. Jerry said no problem, and Cash Apped him the money within five minutes. Bryshere felt like a weight had been lifted off his shoulders. Even though he couldn't get her a gift, he could at least pay for her meal and buy her a few drinks without looking broke in front of her friend. He'd been making sure to calculate every drink he ordered so it wouldn't go over what he had available to spend.

They'd been at Shanghai on the Beach for close to an hour, and the vibe was everything Journey said it would be when she dragged them down there. When Bria came back to the bar from the bathroom, it was as if everything around her was moving in slow motion, and she was the only person in the room. Her thirty-inch weave had been straightened, and she wore a pair of low riding skinny jeans that showed off her hourglass full figure. Her crop top was pink and the material of   satin. It had large Belle sleeves and a deep V-neck to show off her Double D breasts. Her high heels were a soft baby pink, offsetting her clutch purse and accessories. She wore more clothes than half the girls there, but she still put them all to shame. He smiled because his baby was a showstopper.

He watched heads turn and men attempt to grab her hand as she walked towards him. She politely declined and continued over to her seat. Knowing he had the baddest bitch in the room, Bryshere stood to his feet when she approached him, grabbed her by her waist, and kissed her passionately to let them niggas know that she was taken. She happily kissed him back, lacing her arms around his neck. After the very loud public display of affection, Bry pulled out her chair, and she sat down. She was so excited to be out of Atlanta for the first time, she began to do her happy dance in her chair. She had been smiling all day, and he could tell that she was enjoying their trip and her birthday.

"You ordered me another drink, babe?" she asked him while looking at him lovingly.

"I sure did," he replied. "I was waiting for the waitress to come back over so you could order something to eat as well. It's on me, baby," he told her proudly. He hadn't been able to say those words in a long time, and he was happy that he could finally do something nice for his girl. She had been so good to him, and she was always taking care of him. She deserved that same energy to be given back to her.

She blushed as if he had just bought her a Rolls-Royce. She looked so impressed as she reached for the menu. It was obvious to anyone paying attention that he didn't normally treat her. She looked over the seafood selections on the menu until she found what she wanted.

"This lobster tail and rice meal has five stars; I'm going to go with that," she told him while waving the waitress over. After ordering her food, she turned to him to see what he wanted.

"I'm good, babe. I'm still full from all the food we ate earlier," he lied. He didn't have enough money to get them both something to eat and drink. He was going to continue to enjoy the cheap five dollar drinks and let her get what she wanted to eat since it was her day.

"You sure?" she asked him in disbelief.

"Positive. If I order some food, I'm going to play over it. You know you hate when I don't eat all my food," he reminded her of her biggest pet peeve. As a former foster child, not squandering food was very important to her. If she didn't finish her plate while they were at a restaurant, she was grabbing a to go box with pride. She had spent too many nights hungry to throw food away.

"Ok," she shrugged, while giving the waitress back the menu.

"What are you looking like that for?" he began to tickle her, causing her to laugh hysterically. Her weakness was being tickled, and Bry knew it. She began to laugh so hard, she was falling out of her chair. He stood up to catch her, laughing hysterically as well, and he kissed her forehead and pulled her into a hug. His Bria baby was finally leaving her teenage years behind, and he was witnessing the woman she was blossoming into.

"Ok, Ok, love birds, break it up. The birthday girl hasn't broken a sweat all night, so I'm stealing her." Journey walked over to the bar with the guy she'd been dancing with, walking behind her. He hit hands with another guy, who wasn't sitting too far away from them and took the seat a few seats down. Grabbing Bria by the hand, Journey pulled her out to the dance floor as the DJ was dropping another club anthem.

"*When she make that ass clap think I love her.*" DaBaby's voice blared through the speakers, causing all the girls in the club to get up from their seats.

"*Got that ass and that mouth from her mother.*" When the beat for Meg thee Stallion and DaBaby's song, "Cry Baby" dropped, all the girls began to shake their asses.

Walking out to the center of the dance floor, Bria began

to pop her fat ass in slow motion. She then dropped down and twerked while squatting low. She was killing shit so bad, the other girls began to crowd around her and hype her up. They were pulling out their cameras, recording as she gracefully dropped into a full split while still twerking to the beat.

"I see you, birthday girl!!! Everybody tell Bria Happy Birthday. It's Aries season! All my Aries make some noise!" the DJ hyped the crowd as people cheered and shouted out, 'happy birthday' to Bria.

She felt like a princess. All eyes were on her as she glanced out into the crowd. Noticing that the crowd was becoming too hype, the DJ changed the tempo. He didn't want the college kids to go crazy, so he tried to keep the mood of the room at a steady pace. Whenever he played really hype music, he'd balance it out by mixing in some R&B and slow jams. He began to mix in Chris Brown's song "Under the Influence".

"I don't know what you did, did to me. Your body like wait, speaks to me," Breezy crooned through the speakers. Just like that, he had changed the mood of the crowd, and the city girls became lover girls as they slow grinded on each other and on the men who were coming to the dance floor.

Bria's eyes were closed as the liquor kicked in, putting her in her own world. She released her inhibitions as she danced slowly to the soothing melody. It was as if her body had a mind of its own, and she didn't give a damn who was watching. Suddenly, she felt a pair of hands on her hips as she wound them slowly to the beat.

Shit, one of these niggas is on the drunk shit out here grabbing on me. If Bry catches this, he's going to lose his mind, she thought to herself as she stopped dancing, and her eyes shot open. Turning around to prepare to let the guy down easily, she was surprised to see that it was her man with his arms around her waist. She beamed brightly as she caressed his chest and began to slow dance with him like they were the only people in the room. She worked Bryshere over slowly. She could be as nasty as she wanted to because this was her nigga, not some random guy. She would never see the people in this club again, so it was to hell with their opinions.

"Make you cry like a baby yeah, let's GoPro and make a video," Breezy hyped her as she pushed her boyfriend to the ground and began to straddle him in front of the entire club. She was usually shy and reserved, but after a few shots of Don Julio, she was like an animal out of a cage. She squatted over Bry and worked her hips as she began to mimic riding his dick in front of the crowd. She couldn't wait to get back to the house and fuck his brains out. Bryshere was enjoying himself a little too much as his dick began to get hard. He stood to his feet, while scooping Bria's little ass up. She needed to get some water and food in her pronto. She was drunker than he'd ever seen her, and he liked it. He planned to take her to the room and devour her in every position possible. He caught the envious stares of the other females and the longing looks of the other men. Every nigga in the club wished they were standing in his Jordans after witnessing the show Bria had put on while she was on the dance floor.

They laughed as he carried her back over to the bar and sat her on her stool. Journey was still on the dance floor, grinding with the older guy in her own little world. As the waitress returned with Bria's lobster tails and rice, she began to dig in. Bryshere laughed at her and ordered her a bottle of Evian and another shot of Don. He wanted to bring her down a few notches and douse the fire, but he didn't want to put out the flame. He loved this wild side of her, and he couldn't wait to get her back home to see her get wild on the dick.

"I'll take one more of the $5 drinks I had, and you can close out the tab," he told the waitress as he pulled his card from his wallet.

"Also, bring her a to go plate. There's no way she's going to finish all of that," he laughed. She laughed back with him as she walked over to the bar and printed out the ticket of everything they'd ordered, then went into the back to grab a plastic container.

When she returned, she placed the container on the counter and handed Bryshere the check.

It read, $99.32. He'd made it by the skin of his teeth. He cheered inside while handing the waitress the card. Scooping the food into the container, Bria grabbed the water bottle and polished half of it off in one gulp. She instantly began to look a little better. Water was the answer every time. When Bry looked over at the waitress, his heart began to thump. She wiped the card off on her pants then swiped it through the system. Nothing happened. Taking a deep breath, she walked over to another person and grabbed their receipt and their card. When she tried their purchase, a receipt spit out instantly, and she walked it over to them, smiling and handing them a pen. She then walked back to the register to try Bryshere's purchase again. The same thing happened. He began to panic as he hurriedly pulled out his phone and checked his bank balance. When he saw that he had zero dollars and ten cents in the same account that he'd just had one hundred dollars in an hour ago, he began to feel lightheaded. Looking back at his last transaction, it read, $99.90. Clayton State University Tuition Reimbursement plan. The waitress walked up to him solemnly and said, "Your card was declined".

Chapter Five

When Blessen laid eyes on the girl in the pink cropped top, his heart stopped, and he almost called out Sabrina's name. When she walked over to the guy she was with and kissed him deeply, he was brought back to the reality that the girl was not his dead wife, but boy, did she look like her spitting image. As if fate were playing a cruel joke on him, he wished he'd stayed inside instead of coming out to the bar. He found himself watching the girl, who the DJ had called Bria, even though he tried his hardest not to stare. It was her birthday, and he wondered how old she was turning. She had the figure of a bitch his age, but she looked sort of young in the face.

Watching her interact with her little boyfriend burned Blessen's soul. It was as if he were watching his wife cheat on him, and he wanted so badly to go and wrap his hands around the young punk's throat until he reminded himself that Bria wasn't Sabrina. She was definitely thicker than his dead wife. Sabrina had a nice little shape, but this girl had hips and ass for days, matched with the tiniest waist he'd ever seen on a girl her size. For the first time in a while, Blessen felt his dick stiffen as he watched the girl slow hump all over her little boyfriend. He imagined that it was him she was straddling instead. He would know just what to do with all that ass she had on her.

His heart told him to leave; he was only hurting himself lusting after a young girl who was head over heels in love with her boyfriend. However, his feet wouldn't move as he downed shots of Hennessy. When they made it back to the bar and the waitress tried to run the little boy's card, Blessen almost fainted when she walked back over to him with his card and no receipt. The girl had one meal, and they'd only had a few drinks. How the hell could he have a bitch that fine and not afford to pay for her meal in this cheap ass restaurant? To add insult to injury, it was her birthday! If she was his, he would have her somewhere on an island bent over a balcony, fucking her from the back while she stood on top of rose petals. There was no way in hell this punk would allow this bad ass woman that he'd been kissing on all night, to pay for her own meal on her birthday. Blessen watched the boy scramble and take the card back, while giving the waitress another one to try. She took that card and walked back over to the machine. Blessen watched intensely as the waitress swiped the card once and nothing happened. She then wiped the card on her jeans and swiped it again, and no receipt spit out. Blessen sighed in anguish as she walked back over to the young boy and gave him the second card with the news that it had been declined as well.

"It's ok, baby, I'll pay for it," Bria told him nonchalantly as she reached into her purse and pulled out her wallet. Her boyfriend looked mortified as he held his head down in embarrassment. No longer able to sit there and watch, Blessen stood from his seat and walked over to the couple. "Will you allow me to pay this for the birthday girl?" he asked the young boy, man to man.

"Oh, no thank you; we have it," Bria spoke up quickly as she pulled her card from her wallet.

"I was speaking with the young man, beautiful lady," Blessen told her respectfully as he turned back to Bryshere and looked at him eye to eye.

Bryshere had never been so embarrassed in his life. He couldn't believe that the tuition reimbursement plan had taken his money from his account, and it had only been sitting in there an hour. If he had known that it'd draft so quickly, he would have transferred the money from his Cash App card to Apple Cash so it would be safe. Now he was sitting here looking like a lame ass nigga in front of all these people.

"Consider it prepayment. Tonight, I'm having a party. It's called the Fifty Shades of Red Affair, and I need someone to check coats at the door. I'm always scouting for a few college students to help out, and I pay very well," Blessen lied. He'd come up with that from thin air. He worked with a temp agency to provide staff to work his party every year, but this young man didn't have to know that. Reading people was a gift that Blessen was blessed with. He could tell that this young man would be more willing to take the money if he could work for it instead of having it handed to him. That was an admirable trait, and Blessen was impressed. "Ok, no problem. I'm Bryshere," the boy told him while standing to his feet and sticking his hand out to shake Blessen's hand.

"Blessen Harris," he replied while shaking Bryshere' s hand.

Bria had sat there quietly since he told her to hush while the men were talking. Blessen could also tell that she had grown accustomed to being the man and the woman in their relationship. She was so ready to swoop in and fix the problem, she didn't even know how to sit back and let Bryshere come up with a way to pay the tab on his own like he told her he would.

Handing the waitress his black card, she walked over and began to swipe the card in the machine. It spit out a receipt before she'd even fully swiped it as if to say, "Don't play with him; he is not one of them." She walked back over and handed him the receipt to sign, and he saw it read $99.00. He'd spent more than that to park his damn car with valet. Blessen leaned down to sign his signature on the receipt, and the scent of his cologne floated through Bria's nostrils. Blessen felt that Bryshere should have been ashamed of himself for not being able to afford this cheap ass check when he'd known all year that his woman's birthday was coming up. Handing one of the receipts to the waitress and putting the other one in his pocket, he told her to also ring up his meal and use the same card. He needed a separate receipt because he planned to file the dinner receipt with his accountant and write it off as a business dinner. Since he'd discovered how the rich used the system to get richer, he took advantage of everything he could.

"I overheard the DJ say your name was Bria. I'm Blessen. Nice to meet you and happy birthday," he told Bria as he stuck his hand out for her to shake it. The clock had just struck midnight, and he was technically the first person to tell her on the day of her birthday. As Bria looked at him eye to eye, she couldn't deny that he was attractive. He looked amazing, and he smelled so good. Rich nigga energy oozed from his pores, and she felt small in his presence. She had seen attractive boys at her school, but this nigga was fine as hell. He was giving zaddy vibes, and for the first time in six years, her pussy throbbed for another nigga besides Bryshere. When she stuck out her hand to shake his, his large hand covered her small hand completely. He never broke eye contact as he shook her hand and smiled at her.

She had his dead wife's face, and tears almost sprang to his eyes. His Sabrina had been returned to him.

"Girl, I'm tired as hell." Journey walked up to Blessen, Bryshere, and Bria with Huncho behind her. "I was wondering when your ass was going to get tired. Nigga was about to faint, trying to keep up with you. I'm going to call you the Energizer bunny," he joked.

Blessen still had Bria's hand in his, and when she cleared her throat, he pulled his hand away quickly as if he'd been caught with his hands in the cookie jar before dinner time.

"What do we have here?" Huncho asked as he looked around Blessen to see the young lady whose hand he was just holding.

"Hi, I'm Bria," she introduced herself. "This is my boyfriend, Bryshere, and I can see you've met my friend, Journey," she smiled at Huncho.

He looked at her as if she had some shit on her forehead, and he still hadn't offered his name in return. He was too stunned to speak. He'd heard the saying, everyone looks like somebody, but the fact that this young woman was the spitting image of his best friend's dead wife was creepy as fuck. He was about to ask Blessen if he noticed the resemblance, but he gave him a look that told him to keep his fuckin' mouth shut, so he minded his business. Pulling himself together, he introduced himself to the group.

"I invited them all over to my house for the party later," Blessen told Huncho, looking at him eye to eye, and he could see the mischief written all over his friend's face.

"Great, make sure you get an email address for them so they can RSVP as well as download their digital tickets. Y'all are going to have a blast. It's the biggest event of the year," Huncho went along with whatever Blessen's plan was.

"I've been out there busting sweat with you all night, and I don't get an invite to the party?" Journey asked angrily while shifting all of her weight to one side. Blessen was fucking up his groove because he was going to try to take the fine bitch home and fuck on her. The red party was the only event that his wife came to every year; he couldn't have her in the same room with a bitch he'd just fucked a few hours before.

"I'll send a ticket to your email as well; we wouldn't want to leave you out," Blessen smirked at Huncho being petty. He knew that his friend was bringing his wife to the party, so this girl wouldn't be his piece of ass for tonight.

Huncho shot his best friend a look that could melt ice. He would get his ass back for that one.

"The emails I send to each of you will have the directions to my house, your tickets, the itinerary, and all of the things that aren't allowed on my property," Blessen told the group. "It's themed like a gala, so please dress up. There won't be any casual attire permitted, and most importantly, please wear something red," he started before Journey cut him off. "Well, when you say no casual attire, I assume you're speaking about jeans, but we didn't bring anything from campus besides casual attire. I mean, it's not like we go to fancy parties on the regular," she laughed.

"I mean, if you can't make it," Huncho started before Blessen interjected. "Nonsense. Send me the address where you three will be staying, and I can send my personal stylist over with some selections you can choose from," Blessen shrugged nonchalantly.

"Cool!! We're staying at 2512 Princeton Lakes Parkway," she told him with no hesitation.

"I'll send someone over around three p.m.," he finished the conversation before grabbing his receipt from the waitress and grabbing his food that he'd ordered to go.

"It was nice meeting you," Blessen told the three of them after he'd gotten Bria, Bryshere, and Journey's email addresses to send their tickets and saved the address to where they were staying in the notepad of his phone. He walked out of the door quickly and a few steps ahead of Huncho, not stopping until they'd made it outside.

"Your ass think you slick as a perm, don't you?" Huncho started in on him.

"I have no idea what the hell you are talking about," Blessen ignored him as he reached in his pocket for his keys.

"You know what I don't like about your light-skinned ass? You throw me under the bus for being King Sheisty, when you know your ass is just as grimy. You just mask it better. That damn girl could be Sabrina's twin, so you can drop all this fake nice shit you kicking to them. You have something under your sleeve, and I can smell that shit from a mile away," Huncho checked him as he folded his arms across his chest.

"Nigga, I don't know what the hell you're speaking on. All I know is, you need to take your ass home to your wife," Blessen deflected from the topic just as valet was returning with his whip.

"I'm sure not. I booked a suite at the hotel, and somebody's daughter is about to have her legs pointed at the ceiling," he laughed before hitting hands with Blessen and walking over to his car. Blessen shook his head at his best friend, got into the driver's side of the car, and sped off into the night with a smile on his face. He was counting down the seconds until he laid eyes on Bria again.

Huncho waited until his best friend was down the street to jump into his car and speed off into the opposite direction.

Pulling out his cell phone, he dialed her number, and her voice filled his car as she talked to him over the Bluetooth.

"Where do you want me to pull up?" she asked him sexily. This was what he loved about her. She was a real bitch, and she knew that what they had was purely physical.

"Only the best for you. Meet me at the Westin, thirteenth floor, room 1307," he replied before ending the call. When he made it to the hotel, he pulled into the parking garage and stepped through the doors hurriedly as he rushed to the elevator. He had an eerie feeling that he was being watched, but he didn't give a fuck as he tapped his foot, anxiously waiting for the elevator doors to open. When he finally got on, he rode all the way up to the floor with their most expensive suites and exited the elevator. The suite was lavish, with a large glass shower, a jacuzzi tub, a huge king bed, and a bucket with a bottle of champagne on ice with two glasses lay on the counter. Walking over to the bucket, he popped the cork of Ace of Spades and filled both champagne flutes, while removing his clothes. Ten minutes later like clockwork, there was a soft tap at the door.

When he opened the door, she walked inside and began to kiss him immediately as she undressed.

"Whoa, slow down, kitty kat." He called her the nickname he'd given her while handing her a flute of champagne. She downed it in one gulp and proceeded to rip her clothes off. When she was completely naked, he admired her sexy, young body. Her breasts sat perkily, staring straight at him because childbirth and gravity had yet to pull them downward. Her flat stomach, small waist, wide hips, and long legs made his dick so hard, it was throbbing painfully. He looked in between her legs at her fat, freshly waxed pussy and couldn't wait to put it in his mouth. Picking her up easily, he sat her on the counter where the bucket of champagne had once sat and placed her legs on both sides of his head as he sucked her clit, causing her legs to tremble. He gave her back-to-back orgasms as she squirted in his mouth, and he lapped up every drop of her juices. Pulling her down onto her wobbly legs, he took her out to the balcony and bent her over the rail. Grabbing a handful of her long weave, he wrapped it around his fist and fucked her roughly from the back while she moaned his name loud enough to wake up the whole city.

"MMMhhmm, Daddy, fuck meeeee!" she moaned as she tried to grip the rail to give her strength to handle the back shots he was delivering without mercy. He rubbed her throbbing clit in circular motions, causing her to cum again. When he felt his nut building, he pulled out of her pussy, turned her around roughly, and pushed her to her knees in front of him. He then began to fuck her face, causing her to gag on his dick.

Before he could spill all his cum down her throat, he pulled out and shot his load all over her face and into her hair.

After their sneaky link sexcapade, she showered, got dressed, then slipped out of the door like a thief in the night. Huncho took a long, hot shower and relaxed in the king-sized bed until sleep found him thirty minutes later. They'd been at this for years, and she never disappointed.

Chapter Six

It took a lot of coaxing to get Bryshere's drunk girlfriend and her even drunker friend in Bria's small car. He'd never wished for his four-door Honda so bad in his life. He could have easily opened the back doors and tossed both of their asses in the backseat. Luckily they didn't take Journey's Camaro, Bryshere didn't feel comfortable driving her extra expensive car. If he dented or broke anything in Bria's car, she wouldn't complain.

"Throw that ass, birthday girrlllll!" Journey hyped Bria, causing her to stop and twerk in the middle of him trying to put her and her to go plate in the backseat. Bryshere took deep breath and prayed for patience as he regretted that last shot he'd bought her. Well, the last shot their new rich ass friend had bought her. Bry could look at the older man and tell that he had long money. Instead of envying him, he couldn't wait to get to his party tomorrow to find out what he did for a living. He knew there was power in connections. In the world today, it wasn't about the skills you had or what you knew; it was about *who* you knew.

"I'm about to leave y'all drunk asses right here on the curb, I swear to God!" Bry yelled at the two girls, who were having the time of their lives, twerking to the music that was spilling outside of the club.

"Ok, babe. We'll act right," Bria slurred as she got into the back of the car, and Journey followed as if Bry had ruined the fun. He didn't give a damn. He was tired, tipsy, horny, and annoyed that another nigga had to come and bail him out of yet another situation. Now, he was in debt with his coworker for no damn reason. To add insult to injury, tomorrow was the fifth, and he had to pay the interest on the loan he'd exchanged his title for. He prayed that the manager would give him yet another extension because his car was literally the only thing he owned. It was a gift from his grandmother when he graduated from high school. She'd saved up two of her Social Security checks to surprise him on graduation day with the used car, and he was so happy to have a set of wheels, he didn't give a damn if it was old and painted two different colors.

When they finally made it to the house, Bryshere helped Journey into her room. He then struggled to put a drunken Bria into the bedroom they were sleeping in. He undressed her, put her into one of his big T-shirts, removed her makeup, and placed her large bonnet over her hair. He had witnessed her do it enough times to know he didn't put her hair up as neatly as she did. However, she would be grateful that he had tried when she woke up and her weave wasn't a matted mess.

After taking a hot shower, Bry went into the kitchen and poured up a glass of wine and pulled out his cell phone. He decided to do a little research on Mr. Harris to see what he could dig up. As soon as he googled Blessen's name, his business, the beautiful homes he sold, various interviews in magazines, and even an article in Forbes magazine for being one of the best realtors in the South popped up. This nigga was more paid than Bryshere had thought. He had to be sure to leave a great impression tomorrow. A connection like this could be life changing for him.

When Blessen pulled away from Shanghai on the Beach, he called his private eye. He needed to know everything he could find out about Bria Malone and her boyfriend, Bryshere Durden. He paid top dollar to have the best investigator on his payroll. They had both given him their school email addresses; he now knew their full names and that they attended Clayton State University. After making the call to get full background checks, he was pulling in front of his house. After turning off the car, he sat there for a few minutes to replay the night's events. He was a strategic nigga, so he didn't make a move without thinking it through completely.

He knew that he wanted Bria Malone. Not only was she the spitting image of the woman he was madly in love with, she was also sexy as hell. It had been a while since he'd felt any sort of interest in any woman. He also knew that she had a boyfriend that adored her, but he couldn't afford to court her properly. They seemed to have a strong bond, so it wouldn't be easy to take her from Bryshere. Luckily, Blessen loved a challenge.

∞∞∞

The loud banging at the door woke Bry, Bria, and Journey up the next morning. They were all groggy as hell from the partying and drinking the night before, so they'd slept straight through the morning. When Journey went to open the door, there were three people standing on the opposite side. Two women and a man who was dressed like he'd just stepped off a runway. "Can I help you?" she asked groggily, thinking that it was somebody probably looking for her parents. "Mr. Harris sent us to get you ready for the party tonight. Are you Bria?" the woman asked. It was too early, and the sun was shining too bright. The only thing Journey wanted to do was crawl in her bed, but she didn't foresee that happening any time soon. "No, I'm Journey. Come inside," she told them politely so she could get the beaming sun out of her eyes. The two women each had large bags, and the man had an even bigger suitcase.

"Bria, Bry, wake up! The stylists are here!" she yelled to the back room. She went into the kitchen to get a pot of coffee going. If they felt anything like her, their heads were probably spinning from all the liquor. Bria sulked through the living room like a zombie from the *Night of the Living Dead*, but Bryshere was full of energy. He'd spent half the night doing his homework on Mr. Harris, and he couldn't wait to get back in his presence again.

"Well, aren't you a sight for sore eyes?" the man complimented when he saw Bria. They'd been given strict instructions to pay extra attention to Bria to make sure she looked stunning. One of the women was a makeup artist, and the other one was a hairstylist. The man was the personal shopper, and he had a trunk full of designer dresses to ensure that Bria was the Belle of the Ball.

After Bry, Bria, and Journey freshened up, the glam squad got to work. Bria and Journey tried on countless dresses before they found the perfect ones. Journey decided on a red, sexy, strapless dress by Jean Paul Gaultier. The tag was still attached, and the price of the dress was $1,250.00. She also chose a pair of shoes by Givenchy that were gold and studded with rhinestones. The makeup artist did a really over the top makeup look because her hair and dress were very simple. The hairstylist flat ironed her long tresses to silky straight perfection. Blessen had sent over a few sizes of the same suit because he was unsure of Bryshere' s size. The suit was black with a white button-down shirt inside. For his something red, he finished the look with a red tie. His phone buzzed out of nowhere, like it had been doing all morning, and he rushed to forward the number to the voicemail. Bria noticed, but it was her birthday, and she didn't want any smoke, so she decided to just focus on getting dressed and enjoying this extravagant party.

Bria decided on a long red dress that had a high slit up her thigh and accentuated her curvy figure. The top of the dress was a bustier to cinch her waist and push up her breasts. The bottom was a wide skirt with a long train. She completed the look with gold accessories and a pair of gold, sling back Christian Louboutins. The makeup artist did her makeup very soft and elegant but gave her a dramatic red lip to make her large lips the center of attention. The hairstylist decided to pin her long hair into an elegant updo to show her neck, with a few curled loose ringlets to frame her heart-shaped face.

With only a few hours until the party began, they decided

to relax and have a few shots before they headed over to Blessen's mansion.

People came from all over to attend Blessen's annual party. It really was one of the biggest events of the year. His usually quiet mansion was buzzing with hired staff, caterers, servers, and party goers. Blessen knew that having all of the extra staff would drive Georgia and Raymond crazy, so instead of letting them work that day, he gave them the day off, with the option of attending the party if they wanted to. He worked with a temp agency that sent more than enough helping hands to make sure everything was in order.

Blessen sat in his dressing room while his personal barber cut his hair and trimmed his goatee. He was a ball of nervous energy — not because of all of the money he was set to gain if he sold even one of his properties tonight. He was nervous because he couldn't wait to see Bria all dressed up. He'd hired the best glam squad, and for what they cost, he knew that Bria would be stunning. Besides, they didn't have much work to do; she was already flawless. It had been hard for him to sleep the night before because he couldn't get the image of her twerking all over Bryshere on the dance floor out of his head. A soft tap at his door caused him to come out of his daydream and back to the present.

The barber paused as Blessen shouted for the person to come in. It was his private investigator, Jason. He entered the room and handed Blessen two manilla folders. He then nodded and exited. Jason was strictly business and had already been paid for his services. Ready to dig in to see what he could, Blessen waited patiently for the next thirty minutes so his barber could finish cutting and shaping him before he paid him and sent him on his way. Now that he was alone, he could take his time and go through their files. He went through Bria's file first. The report was so descriptive; it had all of her foster families listed, all of the schools she'd attended, even down to the results of her last pap smear exam. Jason had left no stone unturned. Blessen found out about her part time job at Hooters, as well as the amazing grades she was making. She owned a Volkswagen Beetle, and it was registered in her name with the DMV. He also had the names on her social media accounts. When he finished going through the research, he was even more intrigued by her than he had been before. Turning to Bryshere's file, Blessen began to dig meticulously until he found what he needed to make his plan come to life.

Chapter Seven

"You have got to be fuckin' kidding me!" Bryshere exclaimed a few hours later, when the three of them pulled up to Blessen's mansion. Never in his life had seen a house so huge. When his phone buzzed, he rushed to forward the call before Bria could say something. He knew that not answering the call was suspicious, but this was his business, and he didn't need her rushing in to help like she'd offered to do the other day. He would take the money he was about to make and pay off his debts. Looking back at the house, he admired the entire home from the front gate, and there was still a long driveway to drive up before they were close to the house. He could only imagine how huge it was up close. The large, iron gates were intimidating as hell, and he had multiple guards standing outside. There was a line of cars because security went to each car to look at their tickets to make sure only invited people were entering the house. When the guard made it to their car, he checked each one of their digital tickets. He then checked the car and had them pop the trunk while the other guards checked the other cars.

"They're acting like the president is about to be at this party, the way they're checking people," Bria shook her head as they rode through security. Each one of them was in awe as they drove up the long bridge. After they finally parked and stepped from the car, they had to maneuver around all of the people on the outside, waiting for their ID's to be checked to make sure their names were on the list.

"Hell, he just might be coming to this party. Do you see the cars pulling up? Rolls-Royce, Bentleys, Lamborghinis. The cheapest car that I've seen pull up is the one we got out of. It's a whole lot of money in this motherfucker," Journey joked while twerking. Her smile turned into a frown when she spotted Huncho and some woman hugged up, walking into the mansion. He'd been all over her ass. So close, he probably knew what she ate for lunch yesterday. Now, here he was, all over this woman, acting like the perfect spouse. Men were something else, and she laughed to herself as she rolled her eyes.

When they finally made it inside of the house, there were multiple young men there, checking coats with the exact suit that Bry was wearing. They even wore identical bow ties. "Looks like your tribe's over there," Journey joked while pointing to the group of boys.

"Ok, I'm going to head over there and get acquainted. Have fun, ladies. Babe, if I haven't told you today, you look amazing," Bry told Bria as he leaned down to kiss her. He then ran over to the group of boys and introduced himself.

"Now that the ball and chain is occupied, let's go work the room," Journey told Bria while reaching for a glass of champagne from a waiter's tray. Bria followed suit and grabbed one of the fresh-looking strawberries as well and placed it inside of her glass. She felt like royalty being amongst all of these wealthy, powerful people. This time last year, she'd been sitting in a hospital waiting room with Bry, 365 days later, and she was wearing a dress and a pair of shoes that costed more than everything she owned while standing in the same room with millionaires. So much could change in a year. She felt like Cinderella at a ball as she looked around the expensively decorated room. The house was more breathtaking on the inside than it was on the outside. There were crystal chandeliers hanging from the vaulted ceilings, art decorated the walls that looked like they costed more than her tuition for a year. There was a live band playing jazz music as the rich people exchanged conversation. Bria had even caught a glimpse of a few of her favorite celebrities, but she didn't say anything because she didn't want to look like a groupie having a fan moment. She looked like she belonged, and she also had to play the part.

Bria caught the stares and nods of approval from various men, but only one man was bold enough to step to her. She had no idea who the handsome gentleman was who walked up to her and started to randomly chat, but she didn't want to be rude, so she just nodded and smiled.

"I loved you in that game against the Saints, Feleipe," Journey complimented the quarterback for the Atlanta Falcons. "Thank you, I appreciate that," he accepted the compliment before getting back to his conversation with Bria. "It was nice to meet you. I'll be back in a second, Bria." Journey downed her glass of champagne and placed the glass on the nearest table. She'd spotted Huncho alone without the woman hanging all over him, so she wanted to be petty and flirt with him to see him squirm.

Knowing that her man was in the next room, checking coats, Bria attempted to end the conversation with the handsome man, but he just kept on talking. She didn't keep up with sports and had no idea what the hell he was even talking about, but she didn't want to be rude.

"Feleipe Franks, my favorite QB. How are you and the wife liking that house I sold you?" Blessen emerged out of nowhere. He'd been watching Bria since she walked in, and he was impressed. She looked good enough for him to steal her and take her a few feet upstairs to his bedroom and fuck her until she was speaking in another language. It took all of his self-control to contain himself and continue to work the crowd, while still keeping her in his sight. When he noticed that she looked extremely uncomfortable while talking to Feleipe, he went to rescue her from yet another lame nigga who wouldn't know what to do with her if he had an instruction manual. These football players were always conveniently forgetting that they had wives at home when they came to these types of events. They were used to throwing a few football terms around and meeting a desperate server girl who was willing to do anything for a pay day.

"I love it. It's spacious as hell, and she loves it as well. She's hosting these events every other week," he laughed as he mentioned his wife for the first time since he'd started talking Bria's head off.

"Good, I love a happy customer. Stick around, I have some amazing properties I'm going to show in about an hour," he nodded at Feleipe.

"Thanks for coming out, beautiful, you look absolutely stunning." Blessen turned towards Bria and snatched her attention as if the quarterback was as irrelevant as a piece of furniture. Catching the hint that was being thrown, Franks sulked off, in search of the next girl who looked fuckable.

"Not all heroes wear capes. Thank you so much for getting rid of his ass," Bria laughed. She couldn't help but notice that Blessen looked like a work of art. His black suit was tailored to fit his body, and he wore a red, satin shirt underneath. His muscular frame showed through the suit, and his spiked Louis Vuitton loafers had the classic print with red and black designs added. His lingering scent had her in a chokehold. If it were appropriate, she would have asked him if his cologne was called "Bend Me Over". She was ready to stand in front of him and touch her toes. She had to take multiple deep breaths and remind herself that her boyfriend was less than a few feet away, and he could come into the room at any time and catch her drooling at the millionaire who had saved her ass on two separate occasions.

"He does that shit every year, but this time, I can't even blame him. Happy birthday, beautiful. Have a drink with me to celebrate two decades," he told her as he grabbed her hand gently and led her to another room.

"How did you know how old I was?" Alarm bells went off in Bria's head as she gently removed her hand from his.

SHIT, he thought to himself. He'd put his foot in his own

mouth, and he couldn't tell her that he looked into her without creeping her out. "You had to have said it last night while we were drinking. You were faded," he laughed it off, knowing that she wasn't buying what he was selling.

"Thank you for the invite, Blessen, and thank you for everything else. The expensive clothes, the stylists, and more importantly, thank you for giving my man the opportunity to work off his debt to you. However, as I told you last night before you shut me down, I could have paid the tab with no problem," she read him. She didn't want him to think that she was indebted to him just because he had paid a $99 bill and bought some clothes. She had her self-respect, and she wasn't about to flirt or cheat on the man she loved for this man who looked like he ran through women just because he knew he could afford to.

"Excuse me," she told him politely as she turned and walked away.

He smiled broadly. That was his girl. He'd wanted her to turn him down as much as he wanted her to give in to him. Men loved the thrill of the chase, and it only made them want to try that much harder to capture their prey. He would have her because there was nothing he wanted that he couldn't have.

Two hours into the party, the atmosphere had loosened up and was way less stuffy, thanks to the champagne and liquor that flowed freely.

"You can feel free to go grab something to drink and mingle a bit. Around this time, there aren't many people coming in or going out," Marco told Bryshere. He was happy that he was finally getting the opportunity to explore, so he didn't let the boy tell him twice. He wanted to get a stiff drink and find his princess so he could dance with the prettiest girl at the party. In pursuit of Bria, he ran into a waiter first. He reached his hand out to grab a glass of champagne at the same time as a young woman. Neither one of them were paying attention, and their hands locked on the glass in two different spots. When they both realized someone was grabbing for the drink, they let go at the same time, causing it to spill on the waiter.

"AHHH!" the waiter yelped as the drink splashed on him. He then stormed away quickly before either one of them could help him or apologize.

"I'm so damn sorry. I wasn't paying attention," Bry apologized to the girl who looked to be around Bria's age. The youngest people in the party were college students working the event, but he could tell that she wasn't the staff. She looked too damn good. Her light bright complexion complemented her blonde and black hair. She wore it in a fringed bang that framed her face. Unlike the majority of the women in the room, she wore a black dress instead of a red one. It was slinky and fit her body and round ass like a glove. She smiled at him, and he instantly imagined her full lips wrapped his dick.

"No worries, handsome. I'm Jamorie, but I go by Jam. Blessen is my brother. What's your name?" she asked him.

"I'm Bryshere. I go by Bry. Your brother invited me to this party last night. Where do you go to school?" he asked her.

"I'm at Howard University, studying Pre-Law," she retorted.

"Sorry, I stole your drink," she flirted and bit her bottom lip sexily while looking at him.

"It's cool," he smiled back.

"Let's go and get you another one." She grabbed underneath his elbow and walked with him through the corridor.

When Journey finally caught Huncho alone, she finished her second glass of champagne and walked up to him confidently. Sure, her and Liam were a thing, but Huncho didn't know that. The fact that he had gone from hot to cold with her last night was a serious blow to her ego.

So, you are here with who? Your girlfriend? Does she know you were grinding all up on me last night?" Journey questioned

Huncho as he looked around anxiously to make sure his wife wasn't around.

"She's not my girlfriend; she is my wife and the mother of my children," he shut Journey down. He wasn't sure why she was so pressed and all in his business. He hadn't even fucked her last night. If she caused him and his wife to have words about some pussy that she hadn't even given him, he was going to go upside her head. He didn't mind putting his hands on a bitch if she got out of line.

"Calm down, big fella," she laughed, feeling the effects of the champagne kicking in.

"You are worried about who I'm here with like I fucked you last night. Take your young ass to the playroom or something," he spat as his wife walked back up to them.

"Do we have a problem here?" Huncho's wife, Shanna, approached. She was so sick of hoes all over her husband every time she turned around.

She snuck up, startling both of them, and they turned to her guiltily.

"Nah, we're good, baby, there's no problem." Huncho grabbed her around her waist and pulled her in the opposite direction, leaving Journey standing alone, looking desperate.

When the showing of the twelve properties began, Blessen sold three homes and had potential buyers for four others. He had made 2.5 million dollars, and it wasn't even ten o'clock yet. After the business was taken care of, all of the men who liked to gamble followed him up to a private suite in his house that had been converted into a casino. As games of blackjack ran rampant, the men smoked cigars, sipped aged bourbon, and mingled among other wealthy powerful men.

Ready to go to Plan B, Blessen searched the house until he found Bryshere chatting with his little sister. Barging into the conversation, similar to the way he'd cut into Bria and Feleipe's encounter, Blessen invited Bry to gamble with the men, to give them a chance to chat. Excitedly, Bryshere ended the conversation with Jam and followed behind Blessen, like a puppy, into the room.

Reaching into his slack's pocket, Blessen pulled out two $100 bills and handed them to Bryshere. "Thank you for all of your hard work tonight. There's something special about a young man who's willing to work for what he wants, instead of wanting it handed to him." Blessen complimented him while handing him a drink. He smiled and nodded eagerly. The drinks continued to flow and so did the conversation, as Blessen told Bryshere all about the legal side of his business, how hard it was to begin, and shared with him his rags to riches story of coming from nothing and building an empire. Bry had never been more inspired than he was. Blessen offered to take him under his wing as a protégé, and he happily obliged.

An hour later, guests were leaving, but Huncho, Blessen, Bryshere, Journey, Jam, Bria, and a few other people, remained in the gambling room. The women had kicked off their heels as they shot craps and played the slot machines. The men had removed their suit coats, and the atmosphere felt more like a house party as the drinks flowed.

Bria was enjoying herself as she gambled for the first time in her life. She'd even won thirty dollars on the slot machine. Blessen hadn't said anything else to her since his slick comment earlier, and she was glad that he'd gotten the point that she wasn't that type of woman.

"So Bryshere, what do you plan to do with your degree?" Huncho questioned him as they threw the dice on the table. Bry was stressed out of his head because he'd just lost one of the hundred dollar bills that he'd been paid that night. Foolishly, the liquor had made him think he knew how to gamble when he had no idea what the hell he was doing.

"I plan to work in the mayor's office," he replied as he threw another brick and lost twenty more bucks.

"Boooo, there's no money in politics; the money's in real estate," Blessen jumped in and threw his dice on the table, instantly losing the five hundred dollars he'd put up to bet.

"Like I was explaining to Blessen, I don't know the first thing about real estate. Plus, I don't have any money to put down on properties to buy them and resell them. I'm a struggling college student, working for Subway at minimum wage," he laughed at himself.

"Hey, we've all been there. Right, Huncho?" Blessen turned to his friend and asked.

"Hell yes. I was so broke, I couldn't even afford to take my bitch to lunch. Thank God she stuck beside a nigga, and now, we're married and still rocking." Huncho threw the dice and won two hundred dollars.

"How do you get out of a rut like that?" Bryshere asked, taking the bait. He'd never been around so many successful black men, and he was both inspired and intimidated. He was trying to soak up all the game he could to set himself up to be better than he was.

"Well, I went to college and struggled to get my degree. I was down on my dick, struggling to eat and pay that high ass tuition. College is a scam, and a degree is just a piece of paper. I dropped out, found an investor to help me acquire my first property, and it's been up from there," Blessen told half the truth. He'd never gone to college, and he'd never gotten an investor to help him get his first property. He and Huncho had robbed a nigga. Blessen took his half of the money and bought his first property. Huncho blew his on bitches and cars. When he locked eyes with Huncho, his friend smirked because he'd caught the play. Blessen was bluffing, and Bryshere was the mark, but it wasn't money that Blessen was trying to work him out of. It was his bitch.

Chapter Eight

Beads of sweat ran down Bryshere's face as he stepped out on faith and used the last one-hundred-dollar bill he'd made checking coats and placed it on a bet. Blessen had put up five thousand dollars, Huncho put up two thousand, one of Blessen's friends put up fifteen hundred, and the other one put up one thousand dollars. This was the highest bet of the night, and even though Bry knew he couldn't afford to gamble with the big boys, he couldn't let these niggas emasculate him in front of his woman. He had a few too many drinks over his limit, so he was filled with liquid courage. He'd placed the lowest bet at the table, but he was hopeful that he wouldn't lose. After each man rolled the dice and no one was successful in catching a seven or eleven, it was finally Bryshere's turn.

"Come and give me some good luck, baby." He held the dice out in Bria's direction. She moved from her seat next to Journey and waltzed over to her man. Blowing in the dice sexily while never breaking eye contact with him, he smiled at her seductively. Her feminine energy gave him strength he didn't even know he needed. He planted a kiss on her lips, shook the dice in his hand, and threw them on the table with confidence.

When he hit a seven, Bria screamed loudly and gave him a huge hug. Still in slight shock, he didn't realize he'd won all of the money that had been put on the table until all the men began to congratulate him and slide their chips in his direction.

"I'm RICHH! I'm fuckin' RICHHHH!" Bryshere screamed loudly as he jumped up and down like he'd hit the mega millions. Ten thousand dollars was more money than he'd ever seen in his entire life. He'd come to Savannah with nothing but lint in his pocket. He couldn't even afford to put gas in his own car, so he had to leave it and ride with Bria. The title pawn people had been calling him all day long to remind him that his interest payment was past due, but what could he tell them? He didn't have the money, and he couldn't give them something he didn't have. He'd been ignoring their calls and praying that Bria wouldn't ask who it was, so he wouldn't have to lie to her. This money was truly a blessing. He could afford to pay Bria back for all the money he'd borrowed from her. He could afford to pay the title pawn off and repurchase the title of his car. He could afford to pay his grandmother's medical bills and put a little something on his tuition repayment loan so he could finish school. He grabbed Bria and kissed her passionately. If it wasn't for her, he wouldn't have come on the trip, he wouldn't have been at the Shanghai and met Blessen, and he wouldn't have been here at this party. She had been his good luck charm way before she blew on a pair of dice.

"Ok, love birds, break it up," Blessen smiled at them on the outside, even though he was jealous as hell on the inside.

"So, now you can officially afford to play in the big leagues. Let's up the score," Blessen challenged him while shaking his glass of aged Bourbon.

"Scared money doesn't make no money; you know I'm with it," Huncho cosigned.

"I'll put up two hundred thousand dollars, gentlemen. Can anyone match that bet or exceed it?" he asked the men as he looked at each man eye to eye.

"I'll match the bet," one of the other men replied.

"I can't match the bet, but I can put up fifty thousand," the other man with the same accent challenged.

"I can't match that bet either, nigga, but I can match the fifty," Huncho smirked at him, sliding his chips to the center.

The last man left standing was Bryshere. Bria pulled him

away from the betting table so they could talk privately.

"I don't think you should, babe. Let's just take what you won and head out," Bria looked at him fearfully. She didn't want him to play himself and lose everything he'd just won, trying to be greedy. She'd watched enough movies to know that after a big win, there was a bigger loss.

"But Bria, I have the opportunity to win five hundred thousand dollars!" Bryshere whispered to her. He was so excited, his palms were itching, and he could hardly stand still. "That is half a million dollars! I could change our entire lives with that. I can pay off my grandmother's medical bills, I can buy us a house, I can buy us new cars, I can make some investments on property, and have us living like this." He put his arms in the air and waved it around to signify Blessen's mansion. "You always have my back on anything I've ever wanted to do. I need you to let me be the man and support me on this one," Bryshere stressed to Bria as he looked her in the eyes.

She could tell that this was really important to him, and even though she had a sinking feeling in the bottom of her stomach; she nodded her head in approval.

"Are y'all finished discussing?" Blessen asked them while smirking. The fact that he had to talk it over with Bria had Bry fuming inside. She should have trusted him to make decisions for them, and the fact that she didn't, proved that she didn't view him as the King of their relationship. He couldn't blame her; hell, she paid for the majority of the things they did. She was more of the King than he was. That was why he was determined to win this money. When she saw him taking care of her and making grown man moves, she would be forced to fall back and let him lead.

"No discussion necessary; I'm in," Bry retorted cockily.

"That's what I'm talking about, youngblood, that's Alpha energy right there," Blessen hit his hand, hyping him up. Bria felt jaded, but she had to admit; she was proud of Bry for taking control. The only reason she felt the need to overplay her part was because he didn't make her feel like he could handle his role. She had no problem being submissive if he gave her something to submit to. Sitting back on the barstool next to Journey, she picked up her dirty martini and took a sip of it while watching her man handle his business.

"It's almost midnight, and this will be the last game of the night, fellas. Let's do this gentlemen, first roller," the bet runner pointed at one of Blessen's friends, who put up fifty thousand dollars. The man shook the dice feverishly and released them on the table while snapping his fingers. When they landed on a four and two, he gritted his teeth angrily, pushed the chips in the center, and stormed out of the room. He'd just lost all of his money and didn't have anything else to bet.

Blessen, Huncho, and the man who bet one hundred thousand dollars laughed. Bryshere didn't laugh because if he'd just lost fifty thousand dollars, he'd be jumping off a bridge.

"My cousin is a sore loser. I told him to only bet what he could afford," the other man replied with a thick African accent. Next up was Huncho. He rolled the dice and lost. "I see how bruh felt; that's some bull," he shook his head and went over to take a seat next to Jam. He ordered a drink from the bartender and took a few sips when Jam stood up and walked out of the room. He followed behind her, quietly hoping that everyone was too involved in the game to notice.

"And then there were three," the bet runner taunted as Bryshere, Blessen, and the African stood around the table, waiting for their turn.

The African man rolled the dice next. He took his time shaking the dice and transferring them from one hand to another as if he were doing some type of voodoo ritual. He then whispered something into his closed fist and released the dice on the crap table. Each of the dice landed on one, and he smiled.

"I asked my ancestors to let the best man win. Tonight, that wasn't me," he told them in his thick accent. I will be in touch about purchasing the property you have in Ghana. It will be perfect for me and my wives," he told Blessen before patting him on the back and walking out of the door.

"Where is he from?" Bryshere asked Blessen.

"That's Ombola Hinduja. He owns a technology firm in Kenya. He was the richest man in the room," Blessen smirked. "Stick with me, kid, and I'll have you sitting in rooms with people who could change your entire life," Blessen told him.

The next turn was Bryshere's. "Baby, come and give me some luck," he told Bria again. She stood and walked over to his side and blew into the dice. Her entire body was shaking from fear of all he could gain and all he could lose. When she attempted to walk away, he grabbed her hand to keep her next to him. He shook the dice in his hand, clutched his fist together tightly, then released the dice onto the table.

When they finally stopped, one landed on a six, and the other landed on a five.

"CRAP!" the bet runner yelled. He'd just lost his whole ten thousand dollars, and his heart caved in his chest.

"Last but not least," the bet runner turned to Blessen.

"Can I borrow a little of your luck?" he asked Bria.

"As you can see, I'm not that lucky," she retorted as she tried to fight back tears. She'd tried to warn Bryshere about being greedy. Now he was leaving with the same amount he walked in the door with — zero dollars and zero cents.

"I'll take my chances." Blessen held the dice in his fist and pointed them towards Bria. She walked over to him and blew into his fist.

He then released his fist and rolled snake eyes. As if he needed the money, he'd won back everything he lost and then some.

"I'm going to be sick." Bryshere held his mouth and ran off

into the direction of the bathroom. Tears filled Bria's eyes, and she looked down at her watch. It was officially midnight, and her birthday was over. This had gone from the best birthday in the world to her worst nightmare, and she was ready to get the hell out of Blessen's house. Scratch that. She was ready to get the hell out of Savannah period. Being so close to so much money just to go back home to struggle was heartbreaking. She could only imagine what Bryshere was feeling.

"Babe..." She tried to run behind him before Blessen stopped her. "Have another drink, beautiful, and let me speak with him. He will be fine," Blessen assured her as he walked in the direction that Bryshere had gone in. He pulled out his cell phone and sent Huncho, Ombola, and his cousin their money back. They all gambled every year out of fun, so the winner always agreed to return the money. Bryshere didn't have to know that, though. He'd played right into Blessen's hands, and now all he needed to do was close the deal.

He waited for a few minutes outside of the restroom door. He could hear Bry throwing up, and he could also hear him crying his heart out. As if this moment couldn't get any worse, on his way to the restroom, he'd received a notification from the title pawn app that his car had been repossessed due to lack of payment. They'd been calling him all day to warn him that they were about to confiscate the car if he didn't pay, but he hadn't answered to find out that pertinent piece of information.

Now, it was worse than when he started off. He no longer had a car either. This was the lowest point of his life. He slid down the wall in agony and covered his face as he cried. He heard a soft tap on the door, and he assumed it was Bria.

"Come in," he replied angrily. Deep down, he knew he couldn't be angry with her; it was his own fault. She'd warned him to take the money and run, but he let his pride get the best of him.

Surprisingly, when the door opened, it wasn't Bria; it was Blessen.

Reaching for some napkins to quickly wipe his face, he spoke, "I'm sorry for leaving, man. It's just that the money may be nothing to you, but that was everything to me. My car just got repossessed because of a title pawn that I haven't been paying on, my phone bill and car insurance are due, I have a sick grandmother with cancer, and her treatments have to be paid out of pocket monthly, and I probably won't be able to finish my degree because I can't afford to pay for tuition. That money could have helped me out so much," he cried while putting his head in his hands. He no longer gave a fuck about pride or ego, nor did he care what Blessen thought of him. His dick was in the dirt, and he knew for sure that Bria would leave him. Hell, he wished that he could leave himself. He was dead weight, dragging her down like an anchor in a river.

"I know how it is, youngblood," Blessen told him.

"I have the power to help you, but there's something I want in return," he told Bryshere as he washed his hands and used two paper towels to dry them.

Looking up at him with suspense, Bryshere screwed his face up. He knew this nigga wasn't trying him on some gay shit.

"I don't even swing like that, my boy. No offense to the men who do, but that ain't my thing," Bryshere shook his head rapidly. He'd heard of "gay for pay" and knew that there were a few niggas who had slept with rich gay men for the right price, but he wasn't getting fucked for no amount. He didn't give a damn if he had to be homeless and live in a cardboard box; Blessen had him fucked up.

Blessen started laughing hysterically at the fact that Bry thought he wanted him. He laughed so hard, he could barely breathe. While Bry just sat and looked at him stupidly, he spoke when he gained his composure and wiped the tears that had formed in the corner of his eyes.

"With all this pussy in the world, you think I want you? Hell no," he chortled.

"I want Bria," he shrugged nonchalantly as if he'd asked Bryshere for something as simple as a pen and a piece of paper.

Bryshere jumped to his feet and got into Blessen's face. "You just tried the fuck out of me," he gritted, standing face to face with the nigga who'd just disrespected him.

"Calm down. You weren't even this upset when you thought I wanted to fuck you," Blessen laughed while opening his suit jacket and showing Bryshere his exposed .45 hand gun in the waistband of his slacks.

"You're in my house, lil' nigga, surrounded by my people; you wouldn't even make it out of here alive if you touched a hair on my head. Your grandmother, Hattie Mae, would be right behind you," he smiled.

"How do you know my grandmother?" he asked in surprise.

"I know everything about anybody I allow within my home," he retorted.

Looking at him for the first time, Bry could see that Blessen wasn't who he thought he was. He'd assumed that he was a strait-laced real estate mogul and businessman, but now, he could tell that the nigga before him was a street nigga. Blessen was definitely a gangster who had learned how to walk among the sheep without exposing that he was the wolf until the time was necessary.

"First off, Bria would never agree to this. Do you deal in some type of human trafficking shit? I'm not about to sell her to you; she's not property," Bryshere told him.

"Hell no. I deal drugs, not people," Blessen corrected him.

"I don't want you to sell her to me. I want you to loan her to me. One night will do," he smirked.

"So, you want me to let you fuck my girl for one night for five hundred thousand dollars? You crazy as hell." Bryshere looked at him as if he had two heads.

"Is that too low of a number? Everyone has a price; what's yours?" he persisted, while putting his hands in his pockets.

"I'm going to say this one more time. She. Is. Not. Property," Bryshere reiterated.

"Seven hundred thousand," Blessen offered.

"I'm gone." Bry stepped around him to try to exit.

"Eight hundred thousand and your life," Blessen grabbed him by his collar.

"What if she doesn't agree?" Bryshere trembled in fear.

"She'll do anything for you. Convince her," he crossed his arms.

He then pulled out his phone, punched in a few numbers, and Bryshere received a notification. Going to check his bank account, there was a wire transfer for eight hundred thousand dollars. He'd never seen so much money in his life.

He wanted to ask Blessen how he knew his account information, but he'd already answered that question. This nigga knew everything about him. He had no idea how the hell he would get Bria to agree to this bullshit, since he'd been the only man she'd ever been sexually active with.

Jam walked through the halls of her brother's lavish mansion and headed to her bedroom. She loved coming home from college because Blessen lived like a King. She just hated the fact that he treated her like a child. She was eighteen years old and grown enough to make her own decisions. When their parent's died, Blessen went from being a fun big brother to an overbearing father figure. When he ran her first love off, she had decided to get even with him, so she began fucking his best friend Huncho. She knew her brother's right-hand man had feelings for her, but she was just young and enjoying herself with whoever she wanted.

Walking into her bedroom, she went over to the dresser and grabbed the picture of her and her brother's ex wife Sabrina. She missed her sister in law, because she always convinced Blessen to back off and let Jam live her own life.

When her bedroom door opened behind her, it startled her and caused her to look back. It was Huncho sneaking into her bedroom even though her brother was a few rooms away.

"Why the hell would you follow me? Do you want Blessen to find out about this?" Jam asked Huncho angrily. He was getting sloppy, and he knew that if Blessen caught him with his little sister, he would have his head. He'd been fucking Jam since she was fifteen years old, right under his best friend's nose. He didn't care what little punks she'd been messing with since she was away at Howard. Even though he was married, Jam was his.

"Shut up and give me kiss," he told her as he grabbed her by the throat aggressively and put his lips on her. Unable to control himself, he pulled her closer and began to rub all over her body. He was glad that his wife had finally left because he'd been watching Jam like a hawk all night. Sliding his fingers underneath her dress, he began to rub her pussy through her panties. He felt her pussy throbbing, as she began to soak his fingers while moaning in his ear.

"Huncho, we cannn'tttt," she whined as her body said otherwise. She rolled her hips in circles as he slipped two fingers into her wet paradise. "Meet me tonight," he kissed her on her lips. "At our same spot," he kissed her on her neck while sucking softly, causing her eyes to roll to the back of her head.

"MMKAYYY," she moaned as she felt her orgasm building.

"Don't stop, Huncho!" she screamed out as he placed his other hand on her mouth to silence her. She rode his hand until she squirted all over him, making a mess. She couldn't deny that he knew how to please a woman.

"Now we have to get the hell out of here before we get caught" she laughed mischievously as she sucked her pussy juices from his fingers, then she grabbed his hand leading him out the door.

She was blushing and fixing her dress, as Huncho followed her.

"So, what do we have here?" Journey asked as she stood in the hallway with her arms folded across her chest.

She'd watched those two make sneaky eyes at each other all night and slipped out the door behind them when they both left.

"Does Blessen know you're banging his sister?" she smirked.

"That's none of your fucking business." Jam walked into her face, ready to snatch her head off.

Huncho grabbed her by her arm to calm her down. They were young, but he was older, and he knew better. If these bitches got to rumbling, and it got back to Blessen, he was going to want to know what they were fighting for. Journey would tell him out of spite, and the consequences would be fatal.

"What do you want, Journey? What would it take for you to forget what you saw?" Huncho bribed her.

"Well, I just saw you drop fifty bands on a bet in the gambling room, so twenty racks shouldn't hurt you too much," she smiled.

"Bitch, you are going to have to get that twenty in blood," Jam threatened her.

"Chill, I'm going to pay her;" Huncho told Jam.

"No pressure. I'll give it to you by tomorrow, so can we all go back into the room and act normal before shit gets ugly?" he asked both girls.

"Fine by me," Journey laughed, walking back to the room.

"You really about to let this bitch blackmail you?" Jam gritted her teeth.

"Hell no, what the fuck I look like? I'm going to wring that bitch's neck," he whispered in her ear before slapping her ass, causing her to laugh loudly.

When they walked back into the room, everyone had left.

"Where the hell is Bria?" Journey asked while pulling out her cell phone to call her friend.

"Look I'm about to head out. Give me your number, and I'll tell you where to meet me at tomorrow to get your money," Huncho handed Journey his cell phone.

"Remember, don't tell nobody about this shit — not even your little friends." He left the room quickly with Jam right behind him.

"Pick up." Journey tapped her foot nervously as she tried to call Bria back-to-back. She didn't really want the money; she just wanted to fuck with Huncho, but the look in his eyes told her that she'd taken things a little too far. She was ready to get the hell out of Blessen's mansion. Now, she hated that Blessen knew where her parents lived. Playing with powerful people was dangerous, and she didn't want to end up floating in a swamp somewhere. Who knew how determined Huncho was to keep his secret love affair with Blessen's little sister a secret?

Chapter Nine

When Blessen and Bryshere headed back to the room, Bria was the only person left sitting there. She was looking down at her hands sadly, and Bry felt a pang in his gut for what he was about to do.

"Bria, babe, I need to talk to you," he told her while going to sit next to her at the bar.

"Not here, follow me," Blessen told the two of them as he headed out of the door.

"What's going on, Bry?" Bria asked him in confusion. When he left the room, he was gagging, saying he was about to be sick, but now the energy was different. They both followed Blessen to an upper-level deck that they had to climb the stairs to get to.

They were on a rooftop, and you could look over and see part of the large estate. He led them further away into a room that sat with a pool, jacuzzi, pool table, and multiple screen TVs. The room had a cabin-like feel to it, and the large pool was beautiful and in the shape of a B.

Walking over to the minibar, Blessen reached for a bottle of champagne and poured a glass for each of them.

"I will let you talk privately," he told them, while walking out of the glass sliding doors and out near the large pool.

"What's wrong, babe? Are you ok?" she asked him, full of concern.

"I'm fine, Bria," he told her.

Grabbing her hand and rubbing the side of her face, tears

filled his eyes.

"You know I love you more than anything in the world, right?" he questioned.

"Of course, I do, but Bry, you're scaring me," she answered.

"Would you do anything for me, Bria?" he asked her as the tears fell.

"I love you with every part of me, Bryshere Durden. I would die for you. Are you in trouble? We can get out of here right now. I don't care that you lost the money; I still love you. This may be it for now, but shit will get better for us later," she wiped the tears from his eyes.

"Blessen gave me eight hundred thousand dollars, Bria."

"What the fuck did he do that for? What do you have to give him in return?" she asked him with her eyes wide as her hands shook nervously.

"You. I have to give him you," he replied in a low whisper.

"Are you crazy? You can't "give" him me. I'm not for sale. I'm not your damn property!" Bria yelled angrily while hitting Bry in the chest with her closed fist.

"It'll only be for one night, Bria, calm down and listen to me," he begged.

"He wants one night with you. Just one night for almost a million dollars. This money can change our lives. You can let go of that job at Hooters and just focus on school. I will take care of you," he pleaded to her while rubbing the side of her face slowly.

"So, are you my pimp now, Bryshere? If the price is right, you'll just give me to a nigga and let him have his way with me? What if he's into all kind of wild, freaked out shit, and he wants to hurt me, strangle me, fuck me like I'm some useless prostitute? You're ok with that for the right price?" she asked him angrily.

"I would never demean you." Blessen stepped back into the room with his glass of champagne in his hand.

She turned to him and looked him in the eyes.

He walked closer. "You're a lady, Bria, and I would never treat you less than that. I won't hurt a hair on your head; you have my word," he told her as he touched the side of her face gently. She looked down to her feet then turned back to Bryshere.

"Don't make me do this. We don't have everything he has, but we have something he doesn't, and that's love. Don't let him destroy us. Give him his money back, and let's walk out of here with our pride," she told him as tears filled her eyes.

"They repossessed my car, Bria. I'm about to get kicked out of school, and I don't have nothing to my name. If I don't do something, you're going to leave me soon, I just know it," he told her sadly while shaking his head.

"I won't leave. I swear, I won't leave," she promised him. Her heart told her that if she did this, there was no coming back from it, and their relationship would never be the same.

"If you love me, you'll do this," Bryshere told her coldly, avoiding eye contact with her.

Nodding her head, she picked up her glass of champagne and drank the whole thing in one gulp.

She pulled out her phone and texted Journey to go back to her parents' place because she and Bryshere were staying the night.

"Ok, I'll do it," she replied, turning back to Blessen. He smiled at her triumphantly and sipped the rest of his champagne.

Touching the intercom speaker on the wall, Blessen called for Raymond, his butler, to come up to the terrace room. Bria and Bryshere stood in silence as they waited to see what was about to happen next. When Raymond arrived, Blessen asked him to escort Bryshere to his car. Bria was terrified of being left alone with him, but she took a deep breath as she watched him walk away.

When he left the room, Blessen refilled her champagne flute

and began to undress. She wanted to go ahead and get it over with. She felt like a dirty prostitute, but she knew that only she, Blessen, and Bryshere would know about this. She would do anything for Bry, and he needed this money to get out of debt. Blessen could have her body for one night, but she knew who her mind, heart, and soul belonged to.

"Whoa, slow your roll," Blessen laughed while putting his hand on hers to stop her from unzipping the side of her dress.

"I thought maybe you just wanted to go ahead and get it over with," she replied sadly while avoiding eye contact with him.

"Bria, I didn't pay almost a million dollars for pussy. I can get pussy for free," he told her while reaching for her chin and turning her face in his direction. With no choice but to look him in the eyes, he stared back at her, and his eyes were full of longing and kindness.

"We have all night to do that. I'm not in a rush. Follow me. I would like to show you something." He grabbed her by the hand and led her to an elevator, which took them to a rooftop. There was a private jet sitting on the roof with a pilot inside.

"Let's redo your birthday. If you were mine, you wouldn't have begun the day at a cheap ass bar. You would have woken up on an island somewhere. We would have flown in for the party, then we would be on our way back to finish what we started" he licked his lips at her lustfully causing her pussy to get wet. Unable to hold his gaze she looked away.

"I would like to take you to Puerto Rico. I have a beautiful cabana that sits off the coast, and we could be there in a few hours. Or, we can stay here, whatever you are comfortable with," he asked her.

"I can't go out of the country. I don't have any clothes or toiletries; I don't have anything packed," she protested.

"All you need is you, and I'll handle the rest," he told her while pulling her into his arms. Her fear was replaced with a feeling of safety as he held her close. Little did she know, her Spring Break had just begun.

When Bryshere made it to the car, his heart felt heavier with each step he took. He checked his account four times back-to-back. No matter how many times he looked, his balance was still 800,000 dollars. Transferring the money from that account to another account so the money couldn't be touched, he sat in the parking lot for ten minutes as it dawned on him that he was now a rich nigga. Gone were the days he had to put mayo and mustard on a slice of bread because he was too broke to afford meat for a sandwich. He could do what he wanted. He could finish school and help his grandmother. He didn't understand why he had all of this money and still felt empty.

Suddenly, he realized what he'd allowed to happen. He couldn't give his heart to another nigga. Bria was his good luck charm. She'd brought happiness into his life since the day he met her, and she was his person. No amount of money could make up for the fact that she was always there for him when he needed her. Day or night, she would give him the shirt off her back. She uplifted him, stood by him, and loved him when he had nothing. She was priceless. Jumping out of the car, he ran back to the front door and began to bang erratically. The butler, Raymond, opened the door, "Yes sir?" he asked politely.

"Take me back upstairs! I can't let him have her!" Bryshere cried as he tried to get around the butler and back into the house.

"I'm afraid you're too late, Mr. Durden. Blessen and Ms. Bria have already left in his private jet," the butler told him rudely before slamming the door in his face.

He could physically feel his heartbreaking as he picked up his phone to try and call hers. He called back-to-back, and her phone was going straight to voicemail. There was nothing he could do but allow this shit to play out. He hoped that after this was done, she wouldn't treat him differently, but in his heart, he knew that he had made the worst mistake of his life.

THE END

WANT TO INTERACT WITH T'ANN MARIE & HER TEAM? JOIN OUR READERS GROUPS ON FACEBOOK!

T'ANN MARIE PRESENTS: GRANDMA'S HOUSE | Facebook

T'ANN MARIE PRESENTS: GRANDMA'S HOUSE 2.0 | Facebook

WIN PRIZES, BE APART OF LIVE BOOK DISCUSSIONS & MORE!

TMP
TANN MARIE PRESENTS
is now accepting submissions in the following genres

URBAN FICTION * URBAN ROMANCE
STREET LIT * URBAN PARANORMAL
INTERRACIAL ROMANCE

for consideration, please email the first 5
chapters of your manuscript to:

TANNMARIESUBS@GMAIL.COM

www.ingramcontent.com/pod-product-compliance
Lightning Source LLC
Chambersburg PA
CBHW071947120726
48001CB00005B/2066